Dead
On
The
Corridor

Stories And Vignettes From The Mormon Corridor

James Elliott

FIRST PAPERBACK EDITION PUBLISHED 2017.
SECOND PAPERBACK EDITION PUBLISHED 2024

ISBN 978-1-956707-30-4

For my family.

"No story is the same to us after a lapse of time; or rather we who read it are no longer the same interpreters."

—Mary Anne Evans

Contents

Preface

I am surrounded by mountains in every direction. The little valley where I live in the geographical center of Utah was originally inhabited by several Native American tribes, but they were displaced by Mormon Pioneers who fled the United States in the Nineteenth Century for what was then a territory of Mexico. Later, they were joined by thousands of Scandinavian immigrants. Those were my ancestors.

The region was thought to be Zion, and God was thought to be the grand architect.

Here in the most drought-stricken parts of North America, my ancestors clashed with and displaced the tribes; fought wars; experimented with theocracy, polygamy, and communism; built temples, churches, schools. They instilled in their children an apocalyptic mythology; a faith in unique symbols, doctrines, and rituals; a sense of responsibility toward the living and the dead; traditions, food, dialect; and so many other things that still flavor the culture today.

My ancestors established an iron-clad patriarchal system, in which men alone are believed to have the divine authority and power to rule in God's Kingdom, and they embraced a social doctrine that made obedience to their authority the first law of heaven.

But they also established the legendary Mormon work ethic, a social doctrine of charitable service, and the teaching that humanity is a family and all human beings are children of God. The curses and blessings that rise from these traditions are evident today like a city on a hill.

Interstate Fifteen now cuts right through the earliest Mormon settlements, extending from Southern Nevada, through the middle of Utah, and into Idaho.

I am a part of this culture. For better and for worse we are peculiar. The founders of my culture with all their justices, injustices, fears, loves, hatreds, and joys are my parents. And I am their child.

Consecration

The voices of nearly two hundred people rose into the chapel's vaulted ceiling, echoed from its neutral cream walls, and dissipated. The organ crooned along.

A family of latecomers could hear the organ from the parking lot. Mother and father wiped the sweat from their foreheads as they walked across the sunbaked asphalt and stepped onto the sidewalk. Their children ran behind them like a brood of ducklings. They entered through the church's double doors just as the congregation sang the last line of a hymn taken from Job's declaration, "I know that my redeemer lives!"

The hymnals were closed and returned to the wooden slots built into the backs of the pews. Then an old woman offered a rambling invocation.

"Our dear, kind, gracious Heavenly Father. We thank thee for this beautiful day. We thank thee for our good bishop, Bishop Argyle..." She prayed for the bishop's counselors, and for the men who oversaw the bishop, then for everyone on up through the hierarchy of church leadership. She prayed for the nation's leaders, the worlds leaders, and for rain needed to water the parched high desert in which many congregants grew their crops. She prayed for everyone who was suffering, for struggling families, for the homeless. Nearly every soul in the world, living or dead, might have considered itself blessed when she finally said "Amen."

The bishop rose from his seat behind the pulpit. He was in his mid-thirties but seemed a decade younger than he was.

The congregation loved him and smiled up at him as he made the announcements. Outside their meetings they all spoke proudly of him, as if he were their own son, often describing him as *Christlike*. In appearance he did not look like the Jesus depicted in paintings. He was short, built like a bulldog, and his black hair was cut nearly to the scalp. He wore an ill-fitting blue suit and a *Dr. Who* themed tie.

His young wife and three small children sat among the crowd, but the toddler had wandered away from his family, toward the front of the chapel, where a teenaged girl had taken him under her wing.

Before he moved on with the meeting, the bishop had to settle the day's administrative business. When he announced three new Sunday School positions, the congregation raised their hands in unanimous approval.

Down in the benches, young parents distracted their fussing, fidgeting toddlers with snacks, games, coloring books, toys. Babies whined. Women, young and old, paid attention, or wrestled their over-active children into their seats, read their volumes of scripture, or stared at the screens on their phones. Older couples sat close to one another, holding hands. Widows and widowers sat together in cliques, sometimes whispering to each other. All the pleasant scents of colognes, perfumes, deodorants, blended with the chapel's sweet clean scent, creating a smell familiar and comforting to everyone present. Some men and teenaged boys leaned forward with their elbows on their knees, resting their foreheads on the back of the pews in front of them, napping.

A handful of twelve-year-old boys and older teens, the deacons and priests, charged with blessing and offering the sacrament of the Last Supper to the congregation, sat in the front, at attention, with tired eyes.

Most congregants had not taken food or water since dinnertime the night before. This was the first Sunday of the month, when Mormons around the world fasted.

When the bishop finished the administrative matters, there was one last piece of important business to address. This was the reason several families had come from out of town.

"Before we partake of the Sacrament," the bishop said, "we have a very special baby blessing. I'd like to invite Brother Kendall Sanderson to come up with his beautiful baby girl. Also, anyone who has been invited to participate, please come up."

The young father, no older than his early twenties, made his way out of a long bench, shuffling past several pairs of knees. He cradled his infant daughter, whose little white dress flowed far past her tiny feet and hung from her father's arms. She had been sleeping, but in all the jostling she stirred.

A half-dozen other men, grandfathers and uncles, came out from the congregation to the front, just below the pulpit. The bishop, too, stepped down and joined them as they formed a tight circle. Each man had to turn sideways to make room for everyone. The baby's father held her out into the center, and the other men placed their right hands beneath the father's hands. Then each placed his left hand on the right shoulder of the man in front of him.

The baby, who had been fussing, looked at the dark suits and at the mens faces, and began to cry.

"Dear Heavenly Father," began the young father. "By the authority of the Melchizedek Priesthood, we hold this baby in our hands to give her a name and a blessing. The name by which she shall be known upon the records of the church is Diedra Anne Sanderson..." In the prayer that followed he went on to express hopes for his daughter's future, that she would always be surrounded by loved ones, that she would stay true to the faith, that she would grow healthy, strong, intelligent, and that she would make proper life choices. Tender emotions overcame him during the blessing. His voice shook, and he continued through his tears.

In the circle's midst, on the altar made of men's hands, the baby screamed, red-faced, mouth open wide, lips curled. Her arms flailed and her legs kicked frantically beneath the flowing white gown.

Only one minute passed. The blessing was over, and the congregation unanimously responded "Amen." The circle of men parted and went back to their seats. The proud father turned to the crowd and lifted the wailing baby to the view of every eye. People smiled and made various subtle sounds of approval.

By this time, several other babies in the crowd were crying and the chapel's high ceiling dispensed the sound equally into everyone's ears.

The bishop stood again at the pulpit and spoke through the noise. "We'll now prepare for the Sacrament by singing 'God Loved Us So He Sent His Son,' after which the bread and water will be blessed and passed by the young men." He nodded to his left, smiling at the deacons and priests. The boys smiled back.

Then the organ commenced with a prelude.

Covenant

A stocky man wearing a white tank top and white cargo shorts, his dark hair slicked back with ample amounts of hair gel, stood beside an immaculate navy-blue Cadillac sedan that still bore the dealership's plates. The driver's door was open and the man rested one sandaled foot on the doorjamb. Sweat beaded on his brow and he swiped his hand across his forehead, then over his hair, leaving the moistened hair to glisten in the sunlight of the sultry Las Vegas morning.

An older model Buick sedan with an engine that produced a rapid knocking sound had turned from the potholed pavement, through the chain link gate, onto the dry, dusty, pebbled lot. The car came to a stop as far away from the Cadillac as the chain link privacy fence allowed, near the gate. A young man, lanky, clean-cut and clean-shaven, wearing knee-length denim shorts and a red University of Nevada Las Vegas t-shirt, stepped out. And as he warily approached the Cadillac, the slick-haired man began talking.

"What's up? Are you Kyle?"

"Yeah, I'm Kyle."

"What are you, like, twelve?"

Kyle stopped a few steps from the passenger's door and shifted his weight from side to side, then kicked the toe of his right sneaker into the hardened dirt. He moved his arms and hands nervously, clasped them behind him, then in front of him, then at his side, then folded, and then back behind him again. His eyes shifted about.

The older man shook his head. "Just a kid. A scared kid. Really, how old are you?"

"Twenty-one."

The man looked slyly at Kyle, "And, what's your name?"

Kyle, confused, said, "Kyle."

"Nah, that's your *real* name. I'm Dirk. And that's *not* my real name. You got a lot to learn before you can make a run. Get in the car." He motioned to the passenger's side of the car by pointing his chin in its direction. "And when you work for me, you're not twenty-one. You're at least a year over drinking age. You're twenty-two...I guess you'd pass for twenty-two. Get in the car."

Kyle hesitated, and observed the chain link fence, the strands of barbed wire stretched above it, the tan-painted cinderblock building, and the open gate.

"We're gonna burn up out here," Dirk said. "I'll bring you back for your car. Just come on."

Kyle started to say something, but Dirk cut him off.

"Look, you're here because you want to work, right? I'm not gonna stand here and talk about it over the roof of my car. We're gonna get in the car, and I'm gonna tell you about the gig, and then you're gonna get to work. You gotta get in."

Kyle got into the car and buckled up.

Dirk cranked up the air conditioner. "You like this car?"

"Yeah. It's nice."

"She's a brand new CT6 Turbo Luxury." Dirk patted the dashboard. "She's my baby." He put the car into gear and pulled out of the gate onto the dusty gray asphalt street.

Kyle's arms were folded, and he sat rigidly in his seat, looking forward.

"I'm old-school," Dirk said. "Lots of guys like the trucks, but I still say these big luxury cars are the best. I don't care what they say, they're the best."

"It's nice." Kyle said again. His body was tense and his brows were knitted as if he were about to scream.

Dirk pulled the car over into the gravel so he could take his eyes off the road. The sounds of large equipment, dump trucks, backhoes, cranes and cement trucks were all a block away, and it seemed that little section of the industrial district was abandoned.

Kyle stared ahead at a green sign printed with white lettering that read, *The Honest Hoe, Las Vegas Nevada.* Silhouetted on the sign was a naked woman leaning against a backhoe. He averted his eyes to stare at the gravel outside the passenger's window.

Dirk saw Kyle's reaction to the lewd sign. "What's wrong with you? You're a weird kid. Look, you gotta calm down, or I ain't gonna hire you. I can turn around right now, take you back to your car, if that's what you want. Now's your chance."

Kyle did not respond.

Dirk waited several seconds, and said, "C'mon. What'll it be?"

"I'm okay," Kyle said. "I'll do it."

Dirk pulled the car onto the road again and continued driving past the warehouses and brick buildings, toward a stop light.

"Where are you from?"

"I'm from here...I mean, I'm from around here," Kyle said.

"Where around here?"

Kyle stammered. "Gr...Green Valley."

Dirk laughed, cursing under his breath. "Green Valley! You people are supposed to be *buying* this stuff, not *delivering* it." He shook his head and said, "Green Valley...Rich boy wants a piece of the pie."

"I'm not a rich boy."

"Okay, Green Valley."

"I'm not rich. I need the money."

"Listen, you can't be all uptight. It ain't like the movies. Uptight is the kind of thing cops are watching out for. Makes you look guilty. If you have a stick up your ass, you'll get busted."

"Okay. Okay. Sorry."

"So, Green Valley, you can't go around using your real name. You gotta have a *new* name for this. Know why we use fake names?"

"So, the police can't—"

"Nah! The cops 'll figure your name out if they catch you. We use fake names because one of us 'll rat you out. You give all of us a wrong name so we give the cops the wrong name, so the cops can't find you. It's the rats, not the cops, that you need a new name for." Dirk cleared his throat. "So, what's your new name?"

"How about John?"

"John? You wanna get yourself killed?"

"Sorry," Kyle said.

"Sorry? For what?" Dirk thought about it for a moment and said, "We're gonna call you Peter...Pete. A good Bible name. That's your new name.

"But John is a good Bible name."

"We ain't calling you John. You're Pete. Now, what's your new last name?"

"Peterson?" Kyle said.

"Peter Peterson? What's wrong with you?" Dirk cursed. "Your new name is Peter Smith. We'll call you Pete. Okay?"

"Okay."

Dirk turned right at the green light onto a three-lane road and accelerated to the forty-five mile per hour speed limit.

"You're getting in on the ground floor, you know? I just got promoted," Dirk said. "Tim—we called him Tim—he's probably going away forever. You'll probably see him on the news. Anyways, now that he's gone, somebody's gotta take charge of shipping and receiving, right? Might as well be me." He pinched his earlobe and for a moment he seemed afraid. In a whisper he said, "Might as well be me."

"You're new at this?"

"No way! I'm just new in charge, just new as the boss," Dirk said. His face turned red, and his voice shook. "Now, I've been a runner a long time, okay...one of Tim's right hands. I got the longest time on the crew. I know what's up, okay? You're new. You learn from me. And I'm the boss. Got it?"

"Okay, okay. Sorry."

"Why are you always saying *sorry*? Knock it off."

Kyle started to say it again, to apologize for having said it, but he stopped himself mid-word.

Dirk laughed. "Now listen, you know the corridor, right?"

"Corridor?"

"Yeah. We call it the Mormon Corridor."

"I've never heard of it."

"Okay. Well, it starts here in Vegas and follows I-Fifteen all the way up through Utah...all these Mormon towns, like Provo, Ogden and those kinds of places. *That's* the corridor. They got demand there, and we give 'em what they want."

"I've never heard it called that."

"Yeah, the corridor is good money."

"I didn't know." Kyle seemed pained.

"What's the matter? It's just the way it is," Dirk said.

Kyle watched the dashed lines on the road and followed them as one-by-one they blurred past and slipped out of view. He eyed the door's handle, and his right hand began to move toward it. Then he eyed the curb and gutter, the street signs and hydrants and other hazards that could break his body if he leapt from the car. He rested his hand again on his thigh and looked down at his lap.

"So, here's how it works," Dirk said. "At every drop-off point, you're gonna switch cars. That way, every hour or so, you're not driving the same car anymore. Makes it harder to track you down if someone calls the cops."

Dirk reached beneath his seat and passed Kyle a hand-drawn map representing the pointed tip of Nevada, with a jagged red line representing Interstate Fifteen. The line began at Las Vegas and ended near Nevada's southeastern border. *Logandale* was written beside the crude star drawn there. An address was written on the bottom corner of the page, along with a short, scribbled paragraph that described how to find the address.

"You get to Logandale, and they'll be waiting for you. You knock three times...three times. They ask who it is, you say 'Pete,' they come out, you take the bags from your car, throw them in their car, and leave one bag with them. Each bag is marked with its drop-off location. Then they give you a new map and the keys to their car, and you're gone again to the next place, and on and on. You got it?"

"I think so."

"You can't just *think so*. Repeat to me what you're gonna do."

"Drive to this address, knock three times, tell them my name is Pete, transfer the bags to the car, leave one bag, then follow the new map that they'll give me."

"In whose car?"

"In their car."

"Good job. That's it. Lickety split. You drive all day, don't even stop for gas. And if you need to pee, you pull off in the desert somewhere. You get to the last stop, hand off the last bag, and you drive all night back down here, transferring the cars, and you get back to Vegas safe and sound and in your own car. Got it?"

"I think so."

Dirk darted a glance. "You *think so*?"

"No. I've got it."

"Good. Everyone's gonna know Pete's coming, and they're gonna wait for three knocks, and if you ain't Pete and if you don't knock three times, you've blown the transfer. We call the cops. We tell 'em there's a suspicious man outside such-and-such a house. We tell 'em he stole the car. And we tell 'em so they don't figure us out. You get busted, we move some people around in case you rat, then we get us a new Pete Smith. You don't know nobody's names and nobody knows your name and nobody can rat out nobody else by name. Got it?"

"Yeah," Kyle said. "I got it."

"Oh, and don't take your phone. Don't make calls. Don't use GPS to find anything. Tear up the maps after each delivery and get rid of them...Next time you won't need maps. All that stuff's a trail. Don't leave a trail. If you leave a trail and if you lead cops to anybody but yourself, there'll be problems."

Dirk had driven around the industrial district with a series of right turns, and now he turned back onto the road that led to the brick building they started from.

"You got a drug of choice?" Dirk asked. "Along with the cash you get a nice supply between jobs."

"No."

"No?"

"I've never done drugs."

"Never?"

"No."

"You got a favorite liquor? I'll throw in a bottle or two."

"Never drank either."

"What are you, Mormon or something?"

Kyle wiped his palms on his thighs.

"What? Wow! Let me guess. You got home from wherever you missionized, and you took to gambling or you went off to some prostitutes and racked up a debt that you're ashamed of. And it probably ain't even a big debt. I once knew a Mormon kid started running drugs because he owed a thousand on a credit card, he used at the Mustang Ranch!" Dirk laughed. "Anyway, now you're looking for a cash cow to pay the debt. Am I right?"

"You don't know anything about me."

"You're wrong about that," Dirk said. "I know things about you because I've seen it. You don't do drugs, but you wanna run them for quick cash. And you got a debt, and the shame of the debt is worse than the shame of being here running drugs to pay it. Gambling stuff or sex stuff...that's the only reason you guys end up running drugs."

Kyle said nothing.

"Man! When you boys fall, you fall far, don't you? It's good for us though. You Mormon boys are the best runners. I never heard of one that ratted. You do everything you're asked, and you don't get caught, and when you decide you're done, you never rat. You're the best runners. But I gotta be honest, I feel kinda sad to see you here. Almost makes me feel guilty...Almost."

Dirk pulled into the empty stockyard behind the brick building and parked the Cadillac about a car's length in front of Kyle's old Buick. Then he got out and examined Kyle's car. "Maybe when your debt's paid off, you can get a new ride."

Together they transferred seven duffel bags from Dirk's trunk into Kyle's, then Dirk held out his hand. "Okay, give me your phone."

Kyle handed over the phone.

"I'll keep it safe," Dirk said. He pulled off the phone's back, took out the battery, and gave it to Kyle. "See? You keep the battery. I won't mess with your phone while you're gone. It's safe and sound." Then he turned to Kyle's car, "Is that car gonna make it to Logandale?"

"Yeah. It'll be fine."

"Better be, or else—" Dirk made the sound of a siren with his voice and drew circles in the sky with his finger. "Got it?"

Kyle nodded.

"Okay Pete, I'll let 'em know Pete's coming. Follow all the road signs and the speed limit. Knock three times. Say 'Pete

Smith,' get a new map, leave a bag, and everything should go fine. And in the morning, you'll have a pile of cash."

Dirk opened his car door, "Oh, and Pete, if you happen to see people, during transfers or whatever, try and act normal. You know, smile and say *hello* to people and stuff. You're in Mormon-land. If you look all stiff and scared it's suspicious. Okay?"

Before Kyle could answer, the sound of tires rolling across the cracked asphalt and into the gate struck Dirk with a terror that startled Kyle. A large black sports utility vehicle pulled into the yard.

"Go! Go! Go!" Dirk cried. He fell into the front seat of his car and slammed the door.

Kyle did not have time to move. He remained where he was and raised both hands into the air in submission.

The man who got out of the truck was short and balding, with a strip of graying hair around the sides and back of his head. He held a pistol casually, like someone might hold a cold drink. Attached to the pistol's barrel was a silencer.

The man walked toward the Cadillac and pointed the pistol half-heartedly toward Kyle. "You stay there." He approached the driver's side window of Dirk's car. "Whatcha up to Dirk?"

"Ricky," Dirk said, "Ricky, let me explain what's going on. Let me explain real quick, okay? I was just waiting for—"

Ricky fired one shot, and Dirk was silent. The bullet exploded through the door and left a gaping hole surrounded by sharp metal peaks.

Kyle had not moved.

Ricky turned away from the car and walked to where Kyle stood. He slapped the pistol against the thigh of his slacks. Then he flicked his wrist to point the pistol at Kyle's car. "Is that yours?"

"Yes."

"And did Dirk tell you about the stops and the bags and all that?"

"Yes."

"And he's got your phone somewhere in that ridiculous car of his?"

"Yes."

"And you know what'll happen if there's a single hiccup in this whole thing?"

"Yes."

"What's your name?"

"Pete. Pete Smith."

"You done this kind of thing before?"

Kyle eyed the pistol and lied. "Yes."

"Okay," Ricky said. "I'll let them know Pete's coming and someone will meet you back here in the morning. Now, get out of here."

Kyle scrambled to open the car door and fumbled with the keys. He started the car, drove slowly out of the gate, and began his first run on the Mormon Corridor.

Sand Angels

The Saturday afternoon infomercial for kitchen cookery was suddenly interrupted by music that rendered a sense of urgency, and the *Breaking News* reel appeared on the screen. The anchor, with his solid baritone voice, said, "We're interrupting this program to take you live with Karen Conley, in Logandale, where the funeral services for Tyler Matthews will soon be under way."

The cameras then cut to the live link.

The reporter wore a dark pantsuit and a white blouse. Her brown hair was cut to shoulder length and the short warm gusts lifted strands and dropped them just as quickly. Her eyes remained squinted throughout the broadcast, in part to protect them from grains of sand hurled by the wind, but also to protect them from the intense Southern Nevada sun.

The Mormon church building was in the background, a large geometric brown and tan stucco and brick building with tall windows and a rectangular spire.

"Today, this little valley is a different place than it was just a few weeks ago," the reporter said.

Photographs of two children appeared on the screen. On the left, a smiling boy, his dark hair cut short and neatly parted. A light reflected off the top left side of each brown pupil. On the right side of the screen was a little girl, or the likeness of a little girl, the artist's impression of what the corpse may have once looked like. The girl, serene, mouth closed, her black curls shimmering as if the artist imagined a heavenly light shining on them.

"By now," the reporter said, "all of us know the faces of these children. Peoples' hearts were broken when Eight News first reported that their bodies were found in the hills west of Logandale, not too far from where we're standing. Tyler Matthews and the child we've come to know as Sweet Jane did not know that they brought thousands of people together, from every walk of life, and every religion, and from all over Southern Nevada and Utah. But that's what happened. For three days search efforts began early in the morning and ended long after dark. The Mormon and Catholic congregations here in the valley organized their efforts at the park right across the street from this church building. The Clark County Sheriff dedicated a dozen officers. Several other agencies provided support."

Footage from the search appeared, showing hundreds of people gathering at the Logandale park, beneath a small pavilion and under the shade of large trees, organizing search efforts.

"A passerby might have thought this little town was hosting a festival," the reporter said, "except for the worry in peoples' faces, and the way parents held their children close to them."

"When two bodies were discovered, there was shock and sadness here in Logandale. Forensics discovered that little Tyler Matthews died while trying to bring Sweet Jane's body home. For this he is thought of by many of us as a hero."

The reporter now stood in front of a large rectangular window that rose vertically from near ground level almost to the church building's eaves.

"For today's services, dozens of people have brought flowers. Those flowers fill the front of the chapel and surround the boy's casket. His father, Scott Matthews, has been allowed a supervised release from the Nevada State Prison today, and he arrived in a police car a short time ago. He and the boy's mother, Maria Matthews, embraced each other outside the prison for the first time in over a year."

"As you can see, the parking lot and the church are packed. There are so many people here that every chair in the church is set up in the overflow, and there are *still* people standing in the hallways and outside the building."

The camera scanned the parking lot, where women in dresses and men in shirts and ties milled about in the hot wind and under the hot sun. A handful of children played on the sidewalks.

"These events have shaken this valley. But people I've talked to said that there's something sacred about all this. The Mormon Bishop told me that if anyone ever doubted the goodness of the people in this valley, that what we've seen in the past few weeks should remove that doubt.

"We now close this sad chapter of this story. For now, the identity of Sweet Jane has yet to be discovered, and nobody has come forward with any useful information. Eight News will continue to bring you any new information that comes in. Live from Logandale, this is Karen Conley reporting for KLVS Eight News."

The end of the report marked the end of daily, and often hourly, coverage of the story about the bodies found in the desert. Within a few days Logandale returned to its routines. Commuters left in the morning and returned in the evening. Children who weren't playing video games played at the pool in the day and in the streets at night. Blood red pomegranates covered feral bushes in abandoned fields and yards, and children broke them over their knees and ate the sweet-sour seeds, returning home with their faces, clothes and hands dyed red. The middays were quiet, except for the ubiquitous buzz of the cicadas. In the evenings, the sounds of lawnmowers and children began like a soft rain and grew louder as temperatures fell. In the hot nights, toads left the irrigation water and hopped in the streets, and bats dropped out of their dark hiding places to hunt. Church parking lots were filled on Sundays, from morning until late afternoon. Cars were hot enough inside to kill a person in thirty minutes, and the leather upholstery was hot enough to burn skin in a few seconds.

Everything was back to normal.

Three Weeks Earlier

Even under the large shade trees in Logandale's park the early August afternoon pushed the temperature past one-hundred degrees. But none of the boys at the birthday party seemed to notice the heat. The eternally buzzing cicadas, the scent of chlorine from the swimming pool across from the park, and the bouncing of the diving board, the splashing and shouting of children, the swamp smells of the muddy stream that flowed nearby, the tickle of flies on the skin, it was all in the background while the children played a game of touch football, darting around each other, and around trees.

Happy Birthday Tyler! was written in glossy blue gel on the birthday cake's smooth white frosting. A Captain America figurine stood next to the large *8* candle.

After the happy birthday song was sung and all the presents were opened, the boys stood around the picnic table to eat cake. Each child speared his slice over and over with his fork, stuffing his mouth full, frequently looking back at the foam football that lay undisturbed in the shade, acting as if it might grow legs and run away. They soon tossed their half-eaten slices in the trash and ran back to their game.

Tyler's mother covered the leftover cake with aluminum foil to keep the flies off. Then she sat beside another woman and wiped cake crumbs from her hands, contemplating each crumb before whisking it away.

She turned to watch her son, who had wandered away from the other boys and now played alone, and said to the woman beside her, "Thanks so much, Jill. You really didn't need to throw a party for him."

"It's no problem at all, Maria. I would do it again anytime." Jill pointed toward another woman who had helped organize the party. She had been cradling her baby and stood by a tree over where the boys were playing. "And I'll bet Melanie over there would do it again too."

"Thank you," Maria said.

A fighter jet from Nellis Air Force Base was crossing the west desert, and broke the sound barrier, producing an earth-shaking sonic explosion. For a moment after the rumble died, the world was silent. Birds and cicadas stopped their noises. The children at the park and the pool were quiet and turned toward the sound. But one by one, starting with the boys at the birthday party, all the sounds of summer returned.

"You know, you're doing a great job, Maria." Jill swatted at a fly.

"I'm not doing a great job. I'm a mess."

"You're not a mess," Jill said. "Life is just messy." A few seconds later she added, "Do you need a priesthood blessing? It could help."

Maria shook her head. "Bishop Allen gave me a blessing a few weeks ago."

"Oh, okay. Good," Jill said.

Maria seemed to watch her son, but she stared at nothing in particular. She occasionally bit her lower lip and let it slide out from between her teeth. "Sometimes I feel like this is all just too much," she said. "I don't think blessings can get me out of all this. It's a grueling life from here on out, hard and sad. Especially for Tyler. I worry for him. Not myself. Only him."

After they sat in silence for several minutes, Jill said, "I don't know how you're feeling right now, Maria. But I believe the Lord will never give us a trial we can't handle. He will make a way."

"I'm not sure he will," Maria said. "When my husband was arrested, he told me everything would be okay, that it was all just a misunderstanding. But it wasn't okay. It hasn't been okay. He even stole from our families. I trusted my husb—" she shook off the word and started again, "I trusted Scott. Then I lost everything. Tyler's all that's left. He's everything. I'm still alive, so

God has at least left me alive to care for Tyler. But I'm not handling it. I can't handle it."

"Maria," Jill said. "I believe angels are around us to bear us up. There are beings, seen, or unseen. Maybe it's the spirit of a grandmother who has died, or it's a friend who's alive. Maybe God sends someone just in time, just when you fall, to catch you and bear you up. Do you believe God is helping you that way?"

"I don't know what I believe about that, or what I believe about anything anymore."

Jill stared at the ground. Maria went on. "I know you're here for me. It means so much to me that you care about Tyler. But I feel nothing. Just, nothing." Maria examined her fingernails absentmindedly. "I don't know what a guardian angel, or the spirit of a dead relative, would even do."

"I don't know, I guess," Jill said. "I think I've felt the presence of spirits, and they've helped me through the hard times."

"I would like to know what that feels like someday," Maria said.

Jill nodded, then sighed. "I'm sorry all this has happened to you, Maria."

"Thank you," Maria said. "Thank you for your kindness."

Maria watched her son for a few more minutes, then checked the time on her phone. "I guess I'd better get going. Can't be late for work."

"Don't worry about a thing," Jill said, standing. She briefly embraced Maria with one arm. "I'll make sure everyone gets home safe."

Maria nodded. She walked across the patches of grass and dirt to the tree where Tyler played alone with some sticks on the dusty ground. He hugged her tightly, smiled, and said, "I love you, mommy!"

"I love you too," she said. Then she walked to the road, climbed into an older model Toyota, and drove to the cafe in Overton where she would wait tables for eight hours.

Melanie had been standing near the boys, pretending to help manage their game. After Maria was gone, she returned to the table and rocked on her hips trying to calm her fussing baby. She whispered to him, gently shushed him, and tried to feed him a bottle.

Jill was wrapping up the leftover cake and piling up the presents, getting ready to put them in her minivan. "Could you see if the root beer is ready?" Jill asked.

Melanie held the baby in one arm and used her free hand to hold a cup while she pressed the dispenser with her thumb. The root beer was dark, bubbly, and overly sweet, the way home-made root beer should be.

"It's perfect," Melanie said. Then she sat down, cradled the baby, and gave him the bottle. "So, how's Maria doing?" Melanie asked.

Jill continued slicing. "She's stressed out."

"Yeah. I guess anyone would be."

They were quiet for a minute. Melanie broke the silence.

"Do you think she really didn't know what her husband was up to?"

"What do you mean?"

"Well, do you think she ever saw what her husband was doing, and wondered if anything seemed a little off? I mean, wouldn't she have looked over the accounts when he was out and about? All that stuff was just sitting there in the house. Wouldn't you have thought it was strange if it was your husband?"

Jill said, "Who knows? I'll believe her for now. It seems the police believe her, or else she'd be in jail too. I worry about Tyler though."

"He's kind of a weird boy," Melanie said. "Look. He doesn't even know how to play with other kids. I don't think he's even interested."

They both watched Tyler while he fiddled with an anthill.

"He's had it rough the last few years," Jill said. "Cut him some slack."

Jill called the boys back to the table and they filled their cups with the bubbly root beer and it dripped down their faces, leaving their cheeks and hands sticky. When they turned on a hose to wash off, they soaked their hair and clothes as well.

Mothers began arriving to pick up their sons, chatted for a few minutes, then loaded their children into sedans and minivans. Jill's son, her toddler, and Tyler were soon the only boys left. Gifts and leftovers were loaded into the minivan. Jill strapped her toddler into his seat, and Tyler buckled his seatbelt.

"Thank you," Tyler said.

"For what, Tyler?"

"For the ride," he said, "And for the party."

Jill watched him in her rearview mirror. He *was* a little strange. But he was good, gentle, and kind. His eyes were earnest. "You're very welcome," she said.

Tyler stared out the car window, lost in his thoughts, remembering what he found that morning. Before the heat of the day, just after sunrise, he had ventured into the desert and into one of the numerous rain gullies carved by rare rainfalls into the packed sand and gravel. Under a stone overhang, where the soft sand floor was seldom exposed to direct sunlight, he found a pool of rainwater in a natural stone pocket. He had cupped the cold green water in his hands and poured it over his head.

The drive to the sitter's house was short, just a few minutes. Jill pulled the minivan into the gravel driveway of a little old block house. A large air conditioning unit with a clanging fan rattled on the roof. She left the engine running and opened the back hatch. Tyler hopped out and stretched his arms around the large box full of gifts, while Jill took the leftover food. Together they walked to the porch.

A woman with long, unkempt gray hair opened the door. She wore a long flannel nightgown and was tethered to an oxygen tank by a clear plastic tube attached to her nose. Cool air blew out of the house. She invited them in, yelling over the high-pitched barks of her terrier and the loud old air conditioner.

"I'd love to come in, but my kids are in the car. We're just here to drop off Tyler."

"Hello Tyler," Betty said. She rustled his hair with her hand. "Come on in."

Tyler stepped into the cold house and knew where to go. Betty had prepared a place just for him, with his own small television and a box full of snacks.

When Jill was gone, Betty asked Tyler about the party, and he recounted a few details. They ate dinner, watched some shows, and fell asleep early, with their televisions turned on. Betty slept in a recliner with her mouth wide open, her bare feet elevated. Tyler was curled up in a chair, his head on the armrest.

Maria came for him a little after midnight.

Ω

Tyler woke up already dressed in yesterday's t-shirt and shorts, pulled on some socks and slipped into his shoes. In the dim glow of a night-light, he cut a slice of leftover birthday cake and wrapped it in foil. After placing the cake in a backpack, he crept out, shut the door and turned the doorknob back into position. His mother would sleep until mid-morning when summer heat would be too intense to stay inside the trailer.

The sun's first rays appeared from behind Bunkerville mountain in the east as Tyler walked on the faded asphalt streets of his neighborhood and turned west. Trailers and cinderblock houses, with their dirt yards and their rickety patios, lined the streets where he lived, in the old part of town. The asphalt gave way to a dusty gravel road that ran along the railroad tracks. Instead of staying on the road, he climbed the basalt embankment, over the rails and down the other side of the tracks. Now he was in the wilderness, heading south.

He traversed undeveloped fringes of valley inhabited by shrubs and mesquite trees, and these gave way to a hem of mostly-barren, dull, salmon-colored hills. Those hills transitioned to rocky gray and brown desert that rolled upward to higher elevations. The desert was dotted with cacti, sagebrush, Mormon tea, deep green creosote bushes and numerous other small plants.

With a stick in his hand, Tyler ambled along, striking at rocks, cacti, and shrubs, imagining himself in swordfights. He stalked lizards, crept upon them, pounced with a cupped hand, but sometimes caught only a bleeding tail that continued to squirm between his fingers.

Despite his zigging and zagging, and his stopping and starting, Tyler had his destination in mind. He hiked along a ridgeline, toward a sloped plateau in the distance. Then, at a point he chose deliberately, he turned down a steep slope into a gully whose otherwise vertical walls had temporarily widened and opened like a funnel.

He squatted and slid on his feet down the slope. An avalanche of small rolling clods followed him until all came to rest on the rocky floor. There he dusted off his shorts and kicked his shoes against a rock, and the breeze carried the dust into the gully's darker shadows. A gust of wind swept down and blew between the walls and made a sound like a mournful groan.

Tyler hesitated before following the flood-path that was, in places, covered with sand, and in other places, covered with riverbed stones. But once he began, he went with careless abandon.

He crawled under boulders that were wedged between the walls above ground and climbed over boulders that had fallen and blocked the way. The walls of compacted gravel and rock rose to twenty feet, narrowing to only an arm's-length wide. Then they became less vertical as the gully widened to become a tiny valley between two sloping hills again.

The sky above was intense, and blue, as he wound his way along the trail of the shaded gully floor. The rocks were cool to the touch and he stopped to hold his body against a boulder, relishing its coolness on his chest and stomach. "Cold as a air conditioner," he whispered. He drew a long breath through his nose to take in the rock's clean mineral scent, then turned around and pressed his back to it. "Cold as a air conditioner."

Then he walked on, holding up his stick to scrape and bounce it on the ravine's walls. He could rarely see more than a few steps ahead because of the curves. And when a new curve opened new views, he wanted to see just around the next bend, and there was always a next bend.

By mid-morning, after many stops and starts, and after numerous diversions, and a handful of lizards caught and released, he arrived at the pocket of water. His tracks from the day before were still there as if he had arrived just moments before to make them.

The pool lay in a natural bowl of smooth white rock. Over many floods, the bottom of the bowl had filled with sand and riverbed stones that formed a beach on one side, dotted with large, rounded rocks. The green water was still, and the light that filtered into the shade showed the boy's reflection darkly when he bent over to look into it.

Tyler took off his shoes and socks and sat on the sand. He ate the slice of birthday cake he had brought, then splashed the water with his feet, and tossed some rocks into it. He lay in the sand and closed his eyes for a moment. A small gust of wind blew across his face, whispering as it continued along between the gray walls into places he had yet to explore. He wiped the sand off his feet and pulled on his socks and shoes. Then he picked up his stick and walked on.

The gully soon widened again and he climbed the steep incline. From the hilltop, he could see everything in the valley, from the reservoir in the north to Lake Mead in the south, and from the mesa in the east to the railroad track he had crossed in the west. He observed the new housing developments with their stucco homes and terra cotta tile roofs. He could see the state road that served as Main Street, home to a restaurant, the post office, the park, the church building, and the swimming pool. He could see the cars moving along but could not hear them or smell their exhaust. He pulled some leaves off a creosote bush, held them to his face and inhaled. The oily leaves smelled like rain.

He climbed back into the ravine. The curving walls soon narrowed and left a thin trail flanked by vertical rocks, which opened into a natural courtyard. There Tyler saw the corpse hanging high on the wall only a few steps away.

The small dried-up body wore a blue dress. It hung by its neck from a thick jute rope, its feet dangling a meter from the gully floor. The skin, shriveled and browned by weather, was tightly wrapped around the bones, the muscles having withered away. The mouth was an open black hole, with the lips pulled back from the teeth to reveal the jawbone. The nose had lost its cartilage, and the eyelids sank into the eye sockets. The black hair and blue dress were bleached from exposure to wind, dust, rain, and many midday suns. Shade was slowly disappearing in the gully as the sun moved overhead, and a sliver of sunlight fell on the dead child's hair. For a moment Tyler thought she moved, as if the sun had brought her back to life, as if her legs would begin kicking, as if her eyelids would open and reveal the dried dark sockets. He observed the curls in her hair, the folds in her leather skin, the overgrown nails of her fingers and toes, the way the mummified cartilage had re-shaped her ears and nose. A breeze rustled the dress.

With his stick, Tyler pushed against a dried foot, and the body rocked slightly against the wall. He said, "Hello," then waited. But there was no response. Then he shouted "Hello!" His voice echoed in the gully, and he shuffled backward, falling over a boulder. He scrambled back to his feet, sure that something would soon appear from out of the dark and narrow crevices around him. But nothing came.

He stared again at the open-mouthed face that smiled down at him. "I'll get you down," he whispered. "I'll get you down."

He dropped the backpack and walked backward with a constant eye on the body until he rounded the bend. Then he ran, feeling that something was pursuing him just outside his periphery. His imagination saw the girl behind him, her bones clacking on the rocks through the leather soles of her feet, and her skeleton hands reaching for him. He felt his heartbeat high in his throat, and his breaths came in fearful, rapid heaves.

Soon, he stumbled back up the hill, slipping, tripping, falling to his hands and knees, and springing back up to continue running along the ridge.

The hillside was steep, and the brittle clay broke apart easily into tiny rolling pieces that fluttered downhill and over the edges of the ravine as he followed the ridgeline. Soon he was looking down at the ancient sage shrub. The rope, twisted and weather-worn, was wrapped around its gnarled and cracked trunk. The loose end of the rope was half-buried and crusted in dried clay.

He sat on the hillside, planted his feet in front of him, and slid to the edge. He tried to look down at the body from above, but the dirt and rocks were too loose, and they slipped out from under his feet and bounced against the rocks below.

He anchored his feet at the base of the sage bush. The rope was tied in a half knot, tightened only by the girl's weight. Careful not to lose his footing, he loosened the knot and pulled the end through.

The dead girl didn't weigh much. He let out a few inches of rope at a time. And when it slackened, he knew the girl had reached the ravine's floor, and he let the end fall.

Then he turned a little too hastily from the edge, the dirt beneath him shifted, and Tyler slipped. He groped for the sage brush but could not hold it and he tumbled over the edge.

His vision was blurred and his head throbbed. Tyler lay on his back, crying. Blood ran down his forehead, into his left eye, past his left ear, and soaked the hair on the side of his head. The blood dripped onto a rock that pillowed his head, then it seeped into the sand.

Someone kneeled over him and caressed his face with a rough, sandpaper hand, whispering a monotone, rasping lullaby with a breath like rotten meat, and with a buzz like a cicada. When Tyler opened his eyes, he saw the dead girl's sunken, dried eye sockets. Her lips were stretched tight across her teeth and curved upward into a smile.

"Hello boy," she said. She raised her arm to point a bony finger at the rock face. Her joints and skin popped and cracked. "You fell from up there," she said. "It's okay. It's okay. Don't cry."

Tyler rolled over, rose clumsily to his feet, and backed up against the rock wall.

The girl turned her attention to the rope that was still tied to her neck. The loose end had fallen in a disorganized jumble beside her. She worked at the knot with her protruding fingernails, and they pulled away from the nail beds, gnarled and broken. She held her hands up to examine them. "Doesn't hurt at all," she said. "Doesn't hurt at all. Mama can fix it. When we get to mama, she can fix it." She stepped toward Tyler. "Can you help me?"

Tyler stepped backward along the wall for a few steps, then turned and fled. The world seemed to spin around him, and the dead girl hobbled behind, dragging the rope, imploring him to stop. He came to the calm green mirror-like pool of water and climbed into a crevice in the rocks. From there he watched the girl approach.

"Please come down. Please," she said. "What's your name?"

"Tyler Antonio Matthews," Tyler whispered.

"My name is Lucy Mitchell," the girl said. "Can you help me?" She tussled with the rope. "Please?" she said. "Then we can go find mama and tell her all about Uncle Jesse."

Tyler climbed down, and leaned for a few moments against the rock wall before he approached. He walked around the pool with intermittent steps and finally came face to face with her. He pulled at one side of the rope until the knot loosened, then drew the end through, loosened the remaining half knot, and let the rope fall.

"Thank you, Tyler," Lucy said. She dropped to her knees in the soft sand, and played in the water with her hands, drew circles, splashed, watched the ripples spread, and then splashed again. "It's like the pond at the park, the one by the trees, where I go with nana."

She lay down on her back and stretched out her arms. "Want to know what happened?" she asked, "Why I was hanging on that rope?"

Tyler nodded.

"My uncle Jesse," she said. "He brought me…'cause I was gonna tell on him."

"Tell on him?" Tyler asked.

"He touched me on my privates," Lucy said. She placed her hands over her eye sockets and groaned. "I was gonna tell mama. But uncle Jesse called me a tattle tale. Tattle tale, tattle tale! And he hit the wall, and he got real mad, yelling, and he hit the fridge and threw a pop can on the floor and it spilled but he didn't pick it up."

Tyler stared.

"Then uncle Jesse, he put me in the car and he drove a long time and then we walked and walked until I started to cry, and he told me to shut up, and I did, but then I started to cry again. He tied me to a rope and pushed me, because I wouldn't shut up. Pushed me because I did, but then I cried again. And I fell asleep on that rope. And then you got me down."

Lucy began stepping from rock to rock, with her arms outstretched to keep balance, trying to keep off the sand. "Let's play hot lava. Do you know how to play hot lava?"

Tyler stepped onto a rock, then looked for another one. "I'm sad for you," he said.

"It's okay." Lucy counted her steps as she moved from rock to rock, "Six…seven…eight …," starting over each time her dry foot slipped from a stone and landed in the sand.

"When we get to my house," Tyler said, "we'll tell my mom. Eight...nine..."

"Yeah," Lucy said. "What's your mama like?"

"Sad"

"Why?" Lucy asked.

"My dad's in jail. So, my mom's sad...nine...*one*."

"Your papa's in jail? eleven...twelve..."

"Uh-huh. Mom says prob'ly for a long time. Four...five..."

"What'd your papa do?"

"Stole money."

"Oh." Lucy continued playing hot lava. "Seven...eight—oops...one...two..."

The children spent no more time dwelling on sad things, but instead found enjoyment in the company of one another. In their shaded oasis, there seemed to be plenty to do. They used sticks and pretended to go fishing. They pretended the little grotto was their house, and they discussed which corner was the living room and which was the kitchen.

Their play ended when Tyler became too tired. "Where's the bedroom," he asked.

Lucy said, "Here, by the water." She drew a rectangle in the sand with a stick.

Tyler took off his shoes and socks, and dug his toes into the sand, then rested his feet in the water. His head hurt. The left side of his face was covered with blood, and the blood dripped from his chin and had soaked his shirt on the left side. It spread from the hem of his shirt onto his denim shorts and spread until it reached his knees.

Lucy sat down beside him and placed her bone-bare, leather feet into the water. "Feels nice," she said.

Tyler did not say anything.

Lucy went on. "Maybe—maybe they can fix my fingers when we get to your mama's house. Then my mama won't be sad when she sees me. I'll be all fixed up. Doesn't even hurt though. I'm a big girl. Doesn't hurt. I'm a brave girl, mama says. That's how I know I can stay home alone in the day."

Tyler weakly tossed pebbles into the water. His eyes fluttered shut. "Uh-huh. You're brave," he said.

"Do you think your mama might be able to find my mama?" she asked.

"Prob'ly."

"Do you think after we're back with our mamas, we can come here sometimes, and play?"

"Prob'ly."

Tyler's head sank forward, then he fell back, into the sand and stared at the rock ceiling of the overhang.

"What's your name again?" Lucy asked.

He was falling asleep, but mumbled, "Tyler — Tyler."

"And my name is Lucy. Did you forget?"

"Uh-huh. Lucy." He closed his eyes and dreamed that he and Lucy played in the sand in the shade of the rock overhang, near the cold pool.

For three days hundreds of people searched the valley, and thousands kept a watchful eye, paying attention to the local news.

Tyler's mother alternated between weeping and catatonia. The leaders and members of her Mormon congregation were constantly present. The countertops of her little trailer filled up with food, and she received hundreds of voice messages from well-meaning church members.

Maria spent the days wandering alone in the desert hills, crying out her son's name. She did not believe, as many rescuers did, that he was kidnapped, or had fallen into the little muddy stream that flowed through the valley toward Lake Mead. She knew the extent of his explorations in the desert after having found numerous rocks, lizard tails, and sticks in his pockets. She believed that he had roamed into the hills and was lost. And she remembered what he had said on the day of his birthday party.

"I found water," he told her.

"You did?"

"Uh-huh. In a cave. And there's a tree, and the bushes are green. And there's a sandy beach."

"Sounds pretty."

"Uh-huh."

So, Maria ventured into the ancient gullies to find a cave that held a pool of water. The narrow ravines were tomb-like, and she felt at any moment that something terrifying might come around the dark bends. But she never found the little pocket of shaded water where her son's body lay.

Other searchers scoured the desert, but nobody guessed how far the boy had wandered, and they too stopped short of finding him.

In the end, a lone hiker wandered into the desert and found the body. It was bloated and stank in the summer heat, even in the shade. The flies swarmed and their larvae squirmed in the wound on the body's skull. And beside the boy lay a female child, mummified by the dry desert air.

The area became a crime scene. Tyler, they discovered, had died from head trauma, after falling into the ravine. But the girl was a different story.

A rope found at the site, and ligature marks embedded in the dried skin of her neck, indicated she was hanged. Investigators found where she had hung, and they estimated she had been there for two years, until Tyler loosened the rope.

They followed Tyler's tracks from the hilltop and down the steep slope, to the sage bush where he had untied the rope and fallen. They found his blood on the rocks below and followed the path he had taken as he dragged the body as far as the water pocket.

An artist attempted to draw a composite image of the girl which was publicized by news media with the hope that someone might know her, but nobody came forward. DNA samples were taken and compared, and missing children archives were scrutinized. If anyone had ever cared for her, they had not reported her missing and never came forward.

$$\Omega$$

"I love the change of seasons," Jill said.

Maria nodded, "Me too. It's not everywhere a person can wear shorts and t-shirt in November." She closed her eyes to sense the desert air. The smell of creosote bush, something like fresh rainfall, filled her lungs. "Do you think—" She could not finish the thought.

"What is it, Maria?"

"Do you think it ever gets easier?"

Jill turned to Maria and took her hand, Maria leaned in, and they embraced and let their tears fall. The sun began to touch the edges of the brown hills in the west.

Maria wiped her cheek with her palm. "Remember that day, at the birthday party?"

Jill nodded, bowed her head, and took a deep breath.

"Do you remember what you said about angels bearing us up, and about God not giving us more than we can handle?"

"I…I do remember saying that. But I—"

"I've been thinking about it. A lot. I wish it were true for me, but that's not important. Tyler is more important. I've prayed every day to know if God sent angels to be with him and comfort him when he died. I just want to know if God is a God of promises, at least for my son."

Jill did not say anything but stared at the ground.

Maria went on. "He was a good boy. He was sad, and lonely. He bore himself up. Part of me thinks there were no angels, that he had to be brave and die all alone."

"He was a good boy, and a strong boy, Maria."

Maria continued, her voice soft, but indignant. "And that little girl. Do you think God sent angels to comfort her when she was hanging there on that rope? Did the angels bear her up? Or was she afraid and alone too? Did God keep his promises to the children? Does he keep his promises at all?" She rubbed her eyes. "I know you can't tell me if he did or didn't. Nobody can. Nobody in the world."

They sat quietly, until after the sun disappeared behind the west hills, until the orange and lavender light shifted from a deep purple to black.

Worth of Souls

Fran Young awoke in the August heat of St. George, Utah, lying on a filthy sweat-soaked quilt. Her brown eyes flickered open to see the tent's thin blue nylon walls with the sun bearing down on them. She vomited onto the quilt, and some of the vomit fell on a few strands of her long unkempt brown hair. She reached to the corner of the tent where a small, dirty replica of Bertel Thorvaldsen's statue *Christus Consolator* lay, and she held it to her chest. "Dear God," she said. "Dear God in heaven, please help me!" She struggled to turn over and get up on her hands and knees.

Fran's meager belongings were strewn together with the trash on the tent's floor. She folded the quilt over to cover the vomit, then she hastily sifted through everything else in the tent, muttering to herself, picking through the Xanax wrappers, Alprazolam bottles and plastic bags that still had a film of white powder inside. They were all empty and she tossed them aside. The search became more frantic, and she turned over the quilt again and again, licked the film off each wrapper or bag, dug into the bottles with a wet finger to get any residual dust that might reside there.

After she searched the tent once, twice, three times, she remained on her hands and knees panting. Then she reached into the backpack and pulled out a clear zipper bag that contained a blood glucose monitor and numerous testing strips.

She slid the test strip into the monitor, lanced her fingertip and scooped up the drop of blood. In a few seconds, the number forty-one appeared on the digital display.

"Forty-one? Not forty-one! Got to get food. Got to get meds," she said, and whined nervously in half-coherent sentences as she pulled on her shoes, buttoned her jeans, and put on a black tank top. In the corner of the tent was a hairbrush, and she dragged it through the gnarls and vomit several times.

When she unzipped the tent, the hot air from outside flowed into the hotter air inside, and she stumbled out into the sun and stood on red dirt among patches of dried yellow grass that had grown fresh in the spring. Stunted trees and desert shrubs surrounded the clearing and kept Fran's little camp hidden from the world.

She zipped up the tent and staggered down the hill. A headache throbbed more painful with each heartbeat, and she pressed her temples to ease the pain.

Branches had grown across the trail and rocks had tumbled into it. Fran tripped and stumbled, and sometimes fell headlong. When she arrived at the trailer park she walked in the middle of the asphalt until she came to the steep embankment that divided the trailers from the business district. She took her first step into the crumbled red rocks and sand, and tumbled, landing on the asphalt below. Then she turned to the front doors of the welfare office only a few dozen steps away.

The welfare office was an uninviting place with a bland cream and gray interior. The giant open space was filled with rows of tiny gray cubicles and gray desks and commercial grade office carpet. The walls were decorated with mandatory government posters that told people about their right to receive the minimum wage if they found work, and the right of disabled people to receive the same services as the able-bodied.

The reception area, open to the public, was quiet and brooding, its silence frequently broken by the sounds of frustrated people. They sat at computers clicking and typing and printing. They sat at tables with their phones to their ears, and waited thirty, forty, or fifty minutes to speak with case workers. They stood in line, waiting to turn in paperwork, or to report new situations, or to complain.

Fran, walked to the front desk, ignoring the line. "Help me! I'm dying!"

Curious heads popped up from behind cubicle walls, clients turned to see the strange woman, children stopped fussing and listened to Fran's shouts.

A worker at the front desk turned his swivel chair to face Fran. He was plump, with fat fingers, fat hands, and fat cheeks that weighed down both sides of his face and gave him a permanent frown. Without making the effort to stand, he pushed with his legs and rolled his chair toward Fran while he admonished her. "We're going to need you to calm down and take your place in the line."

"But I'm dying!"

He wagged a fat finger. "You're not dying. You look just fine. But you'll have to wait your turn. Please get in the back of the line."

"She's tweaking," a young woman in the line said. "She's totally tweaking."

"I'm not tweaking."

"Okay, okay," the worker said. "If you're dying, we'll call an ambulance. If not, then get in line."

Fran went to the back of the line, watched the clock that hung on the wall, and complained each time another minute passed. She scratched at a scab on her arm. A point of fresh blood slowly grew until it formed a drop that drifted down her forearm, leaving a red trail. After twenty minutes, she was next in line.

"How may I help you." The worker acted as if he had not seen her before.

"I need my meds, and I need food."

The worker pulled a tissue from a box on the desk and dangled it in front of her. She took the tissue and wiped the blood from her arm.

"Okay. What's your case number."

She gave him the case number and said, "I turned in an application last month, but I never heard nothing."

"Okay."

"And I need food today, because my blood is forty-one."

"Forty-one?"

"Yeah, forty-one. You know? The sugar?"

The worker scratched his large belly and glanced up at the small, dirty woman in front of him. "Here's the deal, Fran. You turned in an application three months ago, and you never followed through. So, your application was denied. You'll need to reapply."

Fran's face twisted and she sobbed. "But I got diabetes, and they say I got bipolar."

"Who says that?"

"Doctors," Fran said. "And...and I can feel death coming. The darkness is moving into me and it's squeezing my heart. I need help now! I need food now!"

"Maybe you could try the free clinic. It'll be open again on Thursday. Maybe they'll give you some samples to help you get by."

"I'll be dead by Thursday!"

The worker took off his glasses and rubbed his eyes.

"Look, Fran, don't you have anyone? Your family? Your Bishop?"

"I got nobody. Nobody. If I had somebody, I wouldn't be here."

The worker turned his chair back to his computer. "If you've got an emergency, then go to the emergency room. But all I can tell you is you have to turn in a new application if you want our help."

Fran shook her head and staggered away from the desk, and out of the building. She crossed the parking lot, climbed the embankment to the trailer park. Then she walked drunkenly, tripping, falling to her hands and knees, rising again when the pavement burned, looking into the sky with closed eyes to feel the sun's fire on her face, and seeing the fire through her eyelids.

Two small boys watched, sleepy-eyed and red-faced, from the shaded porch of a trailer, until Fran passed through the trailer park and climbed into the red foothills toward the cliffs. When Fran arrived at her sun-bleached blue tent in the tiny clearing, she managed to unzip the door, then tumbled onto the quilt.

There she lay unconscious as the sun moved in the sky, through the evening when the shade of desert shrubs moved on the tent, and on through the sunset with its otherworldly orange radiance on the red earth. Finally, the last glow of the sun disappeared in the west and the sky was dark except for a sliver of moon.

The night had cooled to about ninety degrees Fahrenheit when Fran's eyes flickered open. She lay on her stomach, gasped for air, and watched the tent's wall as it moved wave-like in the warm breeze.

With all her strength, she turned over and stared at the tent's ceiling. She felt around with a hand, found the little *Christus Consolator* statue and held it on her chest.

The breeze touched the shrubs and grasses nearby, whispered through the tent door, whooshed against the plants, hummed mournfully in the rounded natural pockets and crevices in the nearby cliffs. Night birds occasionally flew past, and the flitting of their wings rose then faded in the darkness. A cricket chirped just outside.

By two o'clock in the morning the withdrawal symptoms had subsided. The trembling, the anxiety, the pressure in her chest, all had faded and died. Her stomach rose and fell rhythmically, and the slow ba-bump, ba-bump, of her heart became louder in her head.

For Fran, death came without fear, anxiety or depression. She was at peace, and she remembered something she had heard a long time ago, a concept she had never understood but which other people talked about, like a mystery in a temple into which she was never initiated. *A peace that surpasses understanding.* A smile, just perceptible, passed over her face.

Fran did not see bright lights, tunnels, or angels. Instead, she observed the low moonlight shining through the tent, the desert's nighttime noises, the breeze that continued to flap at the tent walls. The quilt beneath her body cradled her, and scents from the desert floated around her.

With a long exhale Fran took her last breath. Her heart and her thoughts dimmed to nothing.

Ω

St. George Boulevard intersected with Interstate Fifteen at the northeast corner of the valley, then ran in a straight line for almost two miles, east to west. St. George's unwavering linear streets were plotted before the pioneer settlers built their homes, their schools, their stores, their post office, their tabernacle, or their temple. And the interstate cut through it as if a giant sword sliced the city in half at a crooked diagonal.

On an August afternoon when the sun beat down on St. George and the city shimmered from the radiant heat that the ground sent back to the sky, a blue pickup hauling a trailer-load of hay, traveling southwest on the interstate, took the St. George Boulevard exit and pulled into a gas station.

The passenger door opened and a homeless man, who wore a green jacket and a U.S. Army cap, stepped out. He reached into the bed of the truck, hefted out his backpack and slung it over one shoulder. He reached again and lifted out a milk jug with a small amount of water sloshing in it. Then he leaned into the open passenger door and offered his hand to the driver. "Thank you, sir. You are very kind."

The driver was a middle-aged man who wore a red ball-cap, plaid shirt, and jeans. "It was a pleasure to meet you. Thank you for your service to our country."

With that, the homeless man closed the door. The driver pulled the pickup back onto St. George Boulevard, and soon continued southwest on the interstate.

The homeless man walked to the side of the convenience store, leaned his backpack against the stucco wall and filled his milk jug from the water spigot. Then he took a long drink. He did not remove his cap to let the warm breeze sift through his strawberry blonde hair. Nor did he remove his jacket. His red beard protected his face from any relief the breeze may have given. He needed the long sleeves to hide the dark marks on the crook of his left arm, the anterior of his elbow, where he could almost always find the vein. Except for thirst, he seemed unbothered by the dead dry August heat.

He scanned the outskirts of St. George for a good place to set up camp for a day or two, somewhere out of sight, perhaps in the shade. He eyed the nearby red cliffs across the boulevard, on the city's north side. There in the foothills, below the sandstone cliffs, lay a wild area filled with weeds, shrubs and small trees. From there the boulevard was just a short walk away. A tent could stay hidden there with easy access to the city.

But before he could explore the hillside or establish his camp, there was other business to attend to. A woman had come around the corner of the convenience store and walked briskly past him toward her car.

"Excuse me, ma'am," the homeless man said.

The woman took a few more steps before she turned around. She held a thirty-two-ounce fountain drink with tiny drops of condensation already forming on the sides. "Yes?"

"I apologize for the bother, ma'am. Would you happen to know where the SNAP office is?"

"Snap?"

"Yeah. The food stamp office. Do you know if there's one around here?" He set the jug beside his backpack on the cement, then clasped his hands behind his back.

"I don't know," the woman said, "But give me a sec and I'll find out." She walked to her car, placed the drink on the car's roof, opened the door and retrieved her phone. Then she walked back slowly and searched the web, tapping and scrolling with her thumbs. By the time she stood near him she had an answer. She pointed west and gave him directions, explaining that it was probably behind other buildings, hidden up against the red cliffs.

"Awesome," the man said. "Thank you."

Soon the woman's car disappeared into the river of cars that flowed east on the boulevard and the homeless man walked west on the sidewalk, watching the traffic, until he found a brief break to cross into the median and the westbound lanes. Then he continued down the boulevard.

After a few more blocks he turned north, toward the cliffs, on a narrow street that passed between some restaurants to a parking lot filled with cars. He entered a green stucco two-story building, with a sign above the entrance **that read,** *Utah Department of Workforce Services.* There he spent an hour filing an application for government assistance.

He left the building and walked east, climbed an embankment of red sand and sandstone, into a trailer park consisting of two rows of dilapidated single-wide trailers separated by an asphalt lane. He walked along the lane without seeing anyone outside, and he listened to the televisions, the sounds of small children, and the mundane daytime lives of the people inside the trailers. Swamp coolers, with their loud fans, hung out of trailer windows, their water tanks leaking through rusted bolts and the water dripping into the dirt.

The end of the lane opened up to a path into the red foothills. He began climbing toward the patch of shrubs and weeds he had seen from the gas station, which from his vantage point on the hillside was now hidden from his view.

In the steep climb, he began to have a profusion of sweat that soon soaked his clothing and dripped from his chin. When he reached the first small tree, he stopped in its little circle of shade and drank some water from the jug. He gazed down at the boulevard and made plans for his afternoon. The intersection just downhill was perfect for panhandling.

With his right hand, he rubbed the crook of his arm through his jacket, to ease the pain of the bruised circles that ran in a line along the largest blue vein. His body trembled and tears rolled down his cheeks and mingled with the dripping sweat. "Just one more time. Just one."

He identified the places on the boulevard where he would stand and hustle money. In the trailer park below, he had already seen the cars and the porches, spotted the little evidences drug addicts watched for. He would easily find a seller.

"Probably no more than an hour," he said to himself. "Maybe not even that."

Before he continued uphill to find a place to hide his backpack, he stood like a statue and looked out over the valley and seemed to dream a dream.

In every direction he saw the red and black cliffs that surrounded the city like an invading army. Above the east cliffs, with windows like eyes that watched the city below, spacious homes sat on the edge of the broken black rock. His eyes followed the long grid-like streets, where row after row of two-lane roads ran in straight and narrow lines from east to west, and streets intersected them in right angles, running north to south.

A white limestone temple rose above everything else in the valley. It resembled a castle, complete with battlements, as if the builders planned to defend it with rifles, or with cannons, or with bows and arrows. At the southern end of the valley, he saw the Virgin River in the distance, with its warm muddy water.

The interstate cut a winding line through the scene, and sliced the city in half diagonally, severing the south and east from the north and west, carving through the well-plotted blocks. The sounds of cars and trucks speeding along the interstate echoed through the valley, and the low rumble bounced from the cliffs, back into the city.

He closed his eyes, clutched his chest with both hands, inhaled and blew the air out. The sweat continued to flow from every pore. Just an hour, he hoped, and he would feel okay again.

A great shudder began in his chest, then emanated outward so that for a moment his whole body quaked. He wiped his face with his sleeve. "So strange this place," he said. "Strange, and beautiful...and frightening." There was nothing like it where he had come from, or anywhere he had been.

He took another breath of hot desert air, turned away from the city, and continued up the narrow, winding trail, pushing away the branches of weeds and shrubs that had grown across it, and avoiding the loose rocks.

Soon he came to a tiny clearing where a blue tent lay receiving the sun's full wrath. A breeze whispered at the open tent flap. A cloud of flies clamored to get through the thin walls, and flies darted in and out of the door. The buzzing was a high pitched, hypnotic, and constant noise that filled him with dread.

Though he could not see inside the tent, he could smell that it held death. It was a smell he knew better than most people. He knew what a body looked like after it ripened in desert heat and filled up with maggots.

He placed his hand in his pocket and gripped a circular lapel pin that he kept there. The pin was made of a bronze eagle on a green background. It had a black border containing the words *United States Army*. He rubbed his thumb across the face of the pin for several minutes, feeling the curves of the eagle and the sharp corners of letters in the words. And he stared at the tent that smelled of death.

He slid the backpack off his shoulders. It fell to the ground and a small cloud of red dust billowed for a moment around it. With a trembling hand outstretched, he approached the tent, pushed the flap open, and gazed downward. For five minutes, then ten minutes, he stood paralyzed, remembering, seeing, hearing. The flies circled him, and landed on his beard, his nose, his jacket, his pants.

Finally, he let go of the flap, backed away from the tent, sat down on the red dirt, drew his knees up, and buried his face in his hands.

Ω

Two patrol cars stopped at the end of a lane just northeast of St. George Boulevard. The officers stood outside the driver's door of the second car and talked about how to proceed as they looked into the red foothills. The homeless man who discovered the body sat in the second car and leaned forward with his forehead against the back of the driver's seat. He trembled and covered his face with his hands. Outside the door he could hear the two officers talking.

"Paramedics are already on their way," the woman said. Her name tag identified her as *K. Martinez.*

The other officer, a young man, whose tag identified him as *A. Aagard*, fidgeted with his belt. "Okay. So, who's going to—"

"I'll go." Sergeant Martinez said, and she glanced again into the foothills. Then she opened the car door. "Hello sir." Martinez pointed at the hillside and asked, "Is that the right place?"

He raised his head, nodded, and put his head down again.

"And you say it's up closer to the cliffs, right?"

He nodded again.

"Okay. Hang tight." She shut the door. "I'll run up there and make sure we've got the right place."

Officer Aagard sat in his car and cranked up the air conditioner until the knob would go no farther. Then he looked in the rear-view mirror, "Sorry we had to bring you back up here, sir. We'll get you to a safe place shortly, okay?"

The homeless man did not respond.

Officer Martinez walked to the end of the lane and into the brush. Yellow grasses and weeds populated the area closest to the buildings, but soon gave way to desert shrubs and hardier green plants that lived in the dry soil. She was out of breath by the time she smelled the body.

She arrived at the tent, lifted the flap, then backed away and engaged her radio. "Send them my way. We've got a DB up here."

Officer Martinez lifted the flap again and looked at the dead and bloating body and at the little white statue the woman had clung to her chest when she died.

She had one just like it at home on a shelf. Every Mormon student in her high school who graduated from the church's seminary program received one as a gift. Suddenly she recognized the dead woman. Sad and wondering, she shook her head slowly and dropped the tent flap.

From where she stood, she could see the ambulance and fire truck on the boulevard. They turned onto the lane where the cruisers were parked. Soon six people were winding up the trail.

"What's up Martinez?" a paramedic said. "Smells like a nightmare." He looked into the tent. "That's bad. Really bad. What do you bet you'll find five fake IDs and she'll be a Jane Doe for a while?"

"No," said Officer Martinez. "She's from around here. Her name is Fran."

The body remained in the tent while officers investigated the scene throughout the afternoon and into the evening. Men and women in their uniforms climbed up and down the hillside with their black boxes, plastic bags, latex gloves, face masks and smocks. They cordoned the site and worked within their boundary of yellow tape.

When night came, floodlights were carried up the hillside. Moths, beetles, and other strange creatures flew around the lights, bumping into the glass bulbs again and again. Flashlights seemed to float up and down. And when a flashlight shone inside the tent, the whole tent glowed.

Two people in jumpsuits, hoods, and facemasks placed the body in a black bag and laid it on a stretcher, carried it downhill and slid the stretcher into an ambulance. Others dropped Fran's belongings, including her *Christus Consolator* statue, into a large plastic bag, labeled the bag, then carried it away. They took down the old tent, folded up the poles, pulled the stakes, bagged it all up, and tossed it into a vehicle with everything else.

Finally, an officer wadded up the plastic yellow ribbon, and two others carried the floodlights down. In the hour just before sunrise, the last flashlight bobbed along the trail and left the hillside dark but for the moon, the city lights, and the illuminated white temple.

Then all was quiet except for the crickets, the occasional bird, the breeze in the leaves and the grass, and the constant noise of cars and trucks cruising along Interstate Fifteen.

Broken Millstones

Eden Lebaron sat on a cushioned folding chair at the end of a hallway across from the bishop's office in the Fillmore, Utah church building, and she read a large black leather-bound volume of scripture with a cracked binding and worn pages. The book lay open on her lap, and the soft cover curved around each small thigh. Her white hair was pulled back and tied into a bun. The simple dress she wore flowed to her mid-calves, and its sleeves ran to her wrists. Her jewel-like gray-blue eyes looked up from the book when the bishop opened his office door.

Bishop Evan Argyle was in his thirties. His brown hair was cropped so short that it spiked straight out uniformly around his head. His bushy eyebrows had grown together in the center, and their curvature made him look like he was holding back a joyous laugh. He wore a navy-blue suit with the slacks hemmed a little too high. His multicolored tie, on closer inspection, was *Star Wars* themed.

Bishop Argyle said goodbye to the tall teenaged boy he had just interviewed. He shook the boy's hand and said, "Thanks for coming in today, Brother Burningham." Then the boy walked happily around the corner, out of the church doors, and into the August sunlight.

He turned to Eden and smiled broadly. "Come on in Sister Lebaron. I've been looking forward to this visit all week." He offered his hand, then ushered her into his office and invited her to sit in a chair that sat in front of his polished wood desk. While he waited for her to sit down, he made small talk. "That Burningham boy will make a great missionary, don't you think?"

"Oh yes, he'll be a great missionary. An excellent missionary. He's always been a real good boy." She turned her back to the chair and prepared to sit. "Thank you for making time for me today, Evan." Once seated, she placed the large volume of scripture on her lap, then rested her hands, one on top of the other, on the book.

Bishop Argyle pushed aside the books and leadership manuals that lay open in front of him. He clasped his fingers on the desk and looked at Eden inquisitively. "So, Sister Lebaron, my Executive Secretary said you insisted on an interview."

"Now, Evan, you used to call me *grandma* way back when. Remember?"

"I think I was thirteen when I finally understood you weren't another grandma, but just a family friend...I guess you are family, in a way."

"I think of you as family, Evan."

Bishop Argyle tapped a cheap ball-point pen on the desk. "Well, Sister Lebaron, what can I do for you today?"

"Oh, it's nothing urgent." Eden paused. "Well, maybe it's urgent." She chuckled and her eyes squinted shut. "I don't know if anything's urgent no more. I'm eighty-eight. Nothing seems worth the trouble of calling it *urgent.*"

Bishop Argyle rolled his chair forward, folded his arms, and rested his elbows on the edge of the desk. He glanced at the clock, then at a sheet of white paper to his right, where his Sunday afternoon schedule was printed in a single column with back-to-back fifteen-minute interviews. "How can I help you today, Sister Lebaron?"

"I'm here to confess, Evan."

Bishop Argyle suppressed a laugh. "Confess? I don't mean to take it lightly; I just can't imagine—" He did not finish the thought. "I apologize, Sister Lebaron. Please share anything you feel you need to tell me."

"The reason I'm here today, Evan, is because I haven't got much time left on this earth, and there's something no living person knows about me...something from a long time ago, before the interstate run through here, and a long time before you was born, and I think you need to know. Now, I'll be clear, I'm not here for you to consider me worthy or unworthy of eternal blessings. I know my savior, and I'm at peace with him. Anything you say or do can't change that."

Eden's jaw tightened, and she emphasized her next words, rhythmically striking the leather cover of her book with her hand. "But the records on earth, Evan. The records need to be set straight so that the record in heaven is correct. It's about the records. The Lord's book is written on earth by the church, and in the Lord's earthly book there's an entry missing. Now, you know I been on my own, single, since my daughter was a baby. You know I raised her to be faithful, and she went up to Brigham Young University. You know that she was sealed in the temple, and now she's a grandmother herself."

"Yes, I know," the bishop said.

"Would you say I've been blessed in my life, Evan?"

"Of course. You've lived a long and faithful life. You've got grandchildren my age, don't you?" He glanced at his schedule again, then again at the clock that hung on the wall.

"I sure do have grandkids the same age as you, even older," Eden said. "You're thirty-seven years old, right?"

"Thirty-six."

"Goodness where the time goes!"

"Yes, it flies." He waited for Eden to continue, but when she seemed to daydream, he asked, "What confession would you like to make today?"

"Well, something happened about seventy years ago...No, about sixty-eight or sixty-seven years ago, I guess." She paused to think, nodded, and went on. "I broke one of the Ten Commandments...None of them that everybody breaks every so often, like lying. I broke one of the big ones."

"And you never took it up with a bishop before now?"

"No. I never did. And you know why?"

"Why?"

"Because that sin brung me all the blessings in my life. All my very many blessings. The sin was like a forbidden fruit I ate so that my daughter and her children was safe. I was the Lord's hand of mercy and his hand of judgement. And it was a blessing."

"Could you tell me what you're talking about?"

Eden saw the bishop's worried face and said, "Oh, Evan, don't look at me that way. You know me. I'm your Grandma Eden. I known you longer than anyone alive. Me and your grandma used to watch you when you was a baby, when you was crawling around in your diaper. You know me, and I know you. So, don't look at me that way."

Bishop Argyle did not respond.

"Back sixty-eight years ago, when I was just a girl with a baby, I killed my husband. I killed him and I buried him out in the field where we lived, out west of here, out where I-Fifteen runs now. There's some houses out around there now. But it used to be just fields. And that's where I buried him. Nobody knows, not a living soul anyway."

Bishop Argyle tilted his head. "And nobody ever found out? The police? Nobody?"

"Nobody but one other person. And she's been dead a while. The police always just thought he run off. My husband was odd...the war made him crazy. And he had strange ideas about things, about women, about marriage."

Eden coughed, then went on. "Well, after he was gone, his family come to town a lot. They searched, and they harassed police about it, and they was just ignorant with me. They never come close to figuring nothing out, so the police stopped searching before too long. Truth is though, that most people was glad he run off. They thought he hopped a bus and flew the coop. That's what I told them anyhow, and they believed it. I told them he beat up me and the baby, and then off he went. Me and the baby both had the bruises to prove it. So, they just stopped looking for him and stopped coming over to talk to me about it, and whatnot. He was gone to who-knows-where, they thought, and they knew he was crazy enough to up and run. And so, life went on, and I was left to live my life, and he was who-knows-where, crazy and hiding, or something. But the truth is, I killed him."

Bishop Argyle shifted in his seat and coughed into a tissue, then leaned back to toss the tissue into the wastebasket beside his desk. "I don't know what to think about that, Sister Lebaron. I'm not sure I believe it."

"I thought you might not believe it, a little old lady like me doing something like that?"

"I can't imagine you killing anyone."

"Can't you think of anything I maybe would kill for? Could you imagine it might've been the will of God, Evan? Is there anything that might help you imagine it?"

Bishop Argyle thought about the question. "Sure. Self-defense."

"No, Evan. I didn't need to kill him. I could've run off with my baby if I wanted, when he was off to work."

Bishop Argyle picked up the printed schedule. "Excuse me, Sister Lebaron. I'll be right back." He stepped outside the office.

The Executive Secretary, a stocky disheveled older man with a head full of thick disordered salt and pepper hair, stood in the foyer fiddling with his black tie and watching the doors.

"Brother Morgan," Bishop Argyle Said, "I need the next hour of appointments rescheduled."

"Okay," Brother Morgan said, and he hurried into the small clerk's office to make the phone calls.

On the way back to his office, Bishop Argyle passed the man scheduled to be his next appointment. The man heard the exchange between the bishop and the secretary, and he watched with interest as the bishop walked back into his office without even saying *hello*. Before the door swung closed, he saw the gray hair and conservative dress of the venerable Sister Lebaron. She was sitting in front of the bishop's desk. The man tilted his head, and his mouth dropped open as he guessed at the meaning of what had just happened. Then he got up and walked out into the suffocating heat.

Bishop Argyle sat at his desk and asked for more details. Then he listened to Eden's short confession.

"Back in nineteen-fifty-one," she said, "My husband and me lived in a shack..."

Ω

Eden did not know how to stop the baby's crying. Neither swaddling, rocking, feeding, singing, talking, nor anything else, calmed the baby. She had given up on sleep and curled up on a blanket on the cool wood floor to rest, and to perhaps shut her eyes for a moment. Her long straight black hair fell haphazardly on the old wood planks, and she stared at the little light bulb that hung from the ceiling. The baby lay beside her, fussing, crying.

Reynold, his voice high pitched and gravelly, shouted from behind the bedroom's closed door. "Quiet that baby!" When the baby did not stop crying, he said, "I don't care how small she is, Edie. God says, 'Spare the rod, spoil the child'."

Eden heard the bedsprings squeak and pop as her husband got out of bed. She scrambled to her feet, whisked the blanket off the floor, and hurried outside into the August night. She sat on the doorstep and cried and held the swaddled baby close to her chest.

Reynold shouted again from the bedroom, loud enough for Eden to hear. "If you'd let me deal with her, we could both get some sleep." He pounded on the wall, and Eden listened as he climbed back into the noisy bed. "I swear Edie. I swear to whip you both if you don't do something about that baby."

The world around Eden and the baby became quiet except for the crickets, the breeze that shushed through the brush, and the occasional muffled sound of a bedspring as Reynold shifted in his sleep inside the house. The baby nursed for a long time. Then, surrounded by the warm summer night and the calm breeze, Eden and the baby both yielded to sleep, overwhelmed with exhaustion.

Just before sunrise Reynold dressed for his workday. His blue jeans were well faded at the knees and thighs, and his leather work boots were scratched and weathered. He lifted his toolbelt from where it hung on the back of a wood chair in the bedroom and went into the kitchen for breakfast. But breakfast was not waiting for him.

He flopped the tool belt on the table and eyed the canister of quick oats. At the sink, he filled a pan with water, then set it to boil on the electric stove. In a short time, he added a scoop of oats to the pan, and stirred, gripping the spoon so hard that his fist shook. Finally, in a rage, he slammed the spoon onto the table and opened the door to find Eden huddled on the doorstep, asleep, with the baby in her arms.

Reynold seethed his words with a rigid jaw. "Let me tell you, Edie, I'm the husband here. I'm your Adam. I'm the one you obey. I'm the one you help, before any other. Leave the baby and come!"

Eden went into the house, head down, eyes swollen and tired, and she finished cooking the oats, then scrambled some eggs. All the while, she held the baby in one arm.

Reynold gazed at Eden while he ate spoons full of sticky oatmeal and speared the bits of scrambled egg with a fork.

Just before seven o'clock Reynold drove away in his rusted old Ford pickup. It bounced along the dirt road, turned onto the gravel street, and soon disappeared. The noise of the loud puttering engine, the cloud of dust kicked up by the tires, and the smell of black exhaust, soon dissipated.

Eden put the baby in the crib and shut the bedroom door. Then she sat on a ragged little sofa that was pushed up against the wall beside the front door and picked up a volume of scripture that lay on the floor beside the sofa. She opened the book and read out loud, "...Judge not, that ye be not judged. For with the judgment ye judge, ye shall be judged; and with the measure ye mete, it shall be measured to you..."

She studied intensely and stopped every so often to close her eyes and repeat a passage to herself, weighing its significance. She briefly stopped when the baby woke up. But after feeding her and changing her diaper, Eden continued to read.

Ω

Two women stood on the tiny porch of a small new home with a brown asbestos tile roof, yellow wood siding, and white trim. The yard consisted of piles of dirt and rocks, short pieces of lumber, and other debris left behind by the construction crew. In the narrow gravel driveway sat a new 1951 Ford Club Coupe, red, with a chrome-plated strip along each side.

The home sat on a gravel street, flanked by two homes under construction, where crews were busy at work with their saws and hammers, cat's claws, power generators, metal measuring tapes springing back into their cases, the hollow sound of wood striking wood, and voices shouting back and forth over the noise. A third lot across the gravel road was staked with tiny red flags to mark the foundation of a future house. The brush was cleared from the land, but home construction had not begun. The rest of the building lots were nothing more than flat, vacant desert.

To the south and east of the house, the trees and homes of Fillmore's older neighborhoods stood out against wheat and corn fields. The wheat had been cut, and the fields of short yellow stubble contrasted with the fields of green corn stalks. The mountains beyond were dotted with juniper, oak, pine, and outcrops of granite. To the north and west, feral wheat grew in abandoned fields, and the yellow stalks had dropped most of their seeds. Gray-green sagebrush and yellow-flowered rabbitbrush had also moved in and dotted the landscape.

Across an abandoned field from the new home sat a tiny old house, alone and desolate. A poor farmer built the little shack a few generations earlier, and now it was long neglected, but still attracted unlucky penniless renters who needed a place to live. The paint had worn and peeled away from the exterior, leaving the exposed wood to become ash-colored after many summer suns and winter snows. The roof of hand-split pine shakes had also turned gray but had recently been patched in a few places with new pine shingles. A tiny rock chimney on one side of the single gable, blackened from the smoke of countless winter fires, did not release any smoke on that summer day. Just right of the center of the house's south-facing wall was the door, and on either side of the door was a small window, one for each room in the house. Both windows were covered on the inside with white sheets.

The two women on the new porch watched the old house. The younger woman, her brown hair tightly curled, and wearing a knee-length fire-engine-red skirt, white blouse, and black high heels, stood on the second step. She could not have been more than twenty years old, though she wore a large diamond on her ring finger. She wrinkled her nose and stared at the old farmhouse. Her brows were knitted as if pondering a mystery. "I'd never think anybody was there at all, Carolyn," she said. "I wouldn't even use that place for a chicken coop, let alone raise a baby in there. What do you think she does over there all day?"

"I wouldn't know." Carolyn's shoulder length light brown hair was curled out at the ends, and she wore a blue and white flower-print dress with elbow-length sleeves. She stood just outside the door with one hand resting on a stack of boxes piled against the wall, balancing a box full of pots and pans on the railing with her other hand. "I saw them once, when they headed out for church. Aside from that, I've never seen Eden come or go, only her husband. If I hadn't seen them leave for church, I would have guessed Reynold lived there alone."

Carolyn remembered something. "You know, come to think of it, I *have* heard him yell...Scream like a madman, actually."

"Uh-huh. I heard he came back from the war like that, losing his temper, and such. I never seen it at church, though. He's strange at church, but pretty nice. I guess most people are on their best behavior at church." She folded her arms, "Well, what does Reynold scream about?"

"I couldn't make it out. I just heard him, kind of muffled. It's too far away."

"It'd be interesting to know what he yells about," Ruby said. Her eyes brightened, she wanted to gossip. "But that's not all. He's got lots of weird ideas about church, husbands and wives, and polygamy, and things like that. My husband says he's always making odd comments in priesthood meetings. Has your husband mentioned anything?"

"No," Carolyn said.

"Well, I guess you're new to this side of town. We can't expect you to know much yet."

Carolyn said, "I hope he doesn't hit her."

"That's what we're most concerned about. We're worried he might be beating her. It might be more than just yelling going on over there. He don't let her come to Relief Society during the week, just Sacrament on Sunday. And sometimes she don't show up on Sunday neither. The bishop wants us to check up on her."

"That's probably a good idea," Carolyn said.

"But, problem is, nobody can get her to open the door. We go out there, and we hear the baby crying inside, but I think Eden is laying low, hiding. I don't know why she'd want to be rude like that, but that's how it is."

A large raindrop struck Ruby's hand, and to escape the rain, she climbed the last step onto the porch beside Carolyn and watched her car receive several drops before the rainfall abruptly stopped. Then the sun broke through a gap in the clouds, a whipping wind blew across the fields, and a small whirlwind blasted the house and the car with dust.

Ruby scowled. "Oh, dammit!"

Carolyn raised an eyebrow.

"I'm sorry. I shouldn't swear. But I just had it washed. The ground is dry as a bone, and now we get ten drops of rain and a dirty car."

"It's no bother," Carolyn said. She opened the door, dropped the box she had been carrying just inside, and left the door open. Then she ran her fingers through her hair to straighten the wayward windblown strands.

"It's sure brave of you to move out here with all the dust and mud before they done the roads." She watched the raindrops on the car as they began to dry into little round dots of dust. "Anyways, they asked me to ask you if you might pay Eden a visit. You're her closest neighbor, and it makes sense to have you do that. You can just drive over there—" Ruby looked toward the driveway where only one car, Ruby's car, sat. "Or, I guess you can walk, if your husband never bought you your own car. Maybe she'd open the door for you, and maybe you can be neighborly and see if she needs anything. You could take her a loaf of bread or something."

Just then the large raindrops returned and intermittently smacked the surfaces of the car and the house's roof and made little dark spots on the light brown earth. But the storm soon intensified and a deluge descended from dark clouds that had approached Fillmore from the west desert.

"Oh, dear!" Ruby stepped off the porch and the drops pelted her curls and made them bounce. "I've got to go. Wouldn't want to get stuck in the mud out here. Anyways, do you think you could pay her a visit?"

"Sure, I can," Carolyn said.

Ruby walked quickly to the car on her tiptoes to keep her heels out of the dirt, and she protected her hair with both hands.

Soon she backed the car out of the driveway and drove slowly along the gravel road to the paved streets of Fillmore's more established neighborhoods.

Carolyn gave a pleased glance at the clouds that moved with the wind from the west. Then she stepped back into the house and closed the door.

The next day in the heat of the afternoon, Carolyn faced the little gray shack from edge of her yard. She held a warm foil-covered plate with both hands, and the scent of oatmeal raisin cookies floated around her.

Her ten-year-old daughter, who wore a dress of the same print and pattern as Carolyn's, only smaller, called from the porch, "When are you gonna be home, mama?"

Carolyn stepped onto the gravel. "I'll be back soon. I'm just going over there." She pointed the plate in the direction of the little house.

"That scary old place?"

"Yes, that scary old place." Carolyn turned back to the road. "People live there, you know?"

"Uh-huh, I know." Her daughter went back into the house.

It was a hot, sun-filled, August day, intensified by an approaching storm whose clouds still floated far away in the west.

The heat made the sagebrush release its bitter, pleasant scent and it blended with the smell of the junipers that covered the distant hills and flatlands.

The wind whipped at Carolyn's dress and hair as she stepped from the gravel road onto the little dusty dirt path, where the only evidence of yesterday's rain was a bit of wet clay in the deepest ruts. Between the gusts she could hear the low buzz of the power line that hung from the high uneven posts that were installed hastily along the dirt path by the power company decades ago.

The house was surrounded by clutter that Reynold had brought home hoping that he could sell. An old electric oven, a rusted car engine, piles of lumber separated by size and graying in the sun, the ancient countertop from a pharmacy complete with rusted soda dispensers, metal pipes, canvas hoses, broken shelves, a large number of green military ammunition boxes rusted shut, and other odds and ends were all scattered about haphazardly.

Carolyn arrived at the door, an ancient wood slab that had been repaired and painted many times. She placed a foot on the small step, stretched out her arm, and knocked.

She could hear the subtle pop of floorboards inside as someone tiptoed toward the door, and she heard the slightest metallic click from the pressure of fingers on the doorknob. Then she heard the baby whimper.

"Hello?" Carolyn leaned closer to the door. "Eden?"

No answer.

"Eden, I brought cookies. I'll just leave them here." She laid the plate on the doorstep, then backed a few steps away from the door before she turned and walked home.

When she stepped into her driveway she turned to see the solitary little house. This time, Eden stood on the doorstep in a faded yellow dress that hung to her ankles. Her pale face, framed in long dark hair, seemed to watch Carolyn's house. She had picked up the plate, and the sunlight reflected from the foil, and for a moment Eden appeared to hold white flames in her hands.

Carolyn waved.

Eden waved back, then turned around and closed the door behind her.

Ω

Reynold arrived home later that evening and sat rigid in his chair at the small round kitchen table. He opened the Bible in front of him, to the book of Genesis, and read. He only moved to turn pages. His tense fists rested on the table.

Eden prepared dinner cradling the wide-eyed baby in one arm, using her free hand to move the pan to and from the stovetop, to stir the food with a wood spoon, and to add oil, salt, and pepper. A smoky haze filled the house, and slowly floated out the open back door. Soon she piled chunks of ham and pan-fried potatoes on a plate and set the plate in front of Reynold. Then she poured a glass of water and set the glass and a fork beside the plate.

Reynold remained motionless in the chair, furrowed brows, staring tight-lipped, frowning, reading Genesis until the food was cold and the sun fell below the desert horizon.

At just after nine o'clock he left the table without eating, and walked into the bedroom, stiff-legged, arms at his side, like a man in a trance. Eden sat on the bed breastfeeding the half-asleep baby. She hunched submissively and watched Reynold in her periphery. The thick sheet covering the window filtered just enough of the dusky light to illuminate Reynold's bitter anger, and his clenched fists, and the ripples of veins and tendons on his arms and his neck.

"Put the baby in the crib, Edie," Reynold said.

"But she's not sleeping yet, just give me a—"

"Now!" Reynold slammed the door and startled the baby.

Eden laid the baby in the crib, and while she was still bent over to tuck her in, Reynold took a fistful of her hair, pulled her backward, and flung her onto the bed.

"You stay there." He pointed at her. "Obedience, Edie. You will obey me as I obey God." Reynold gripped the bars of the crib and dragged it viciously to the door. But it was too wide to pass through the doorway without removing the door from its hinges, and its bars cracked and splintered as Reynold tried to force it through. The baby reached her arms out and screamed in terror.

He soon gave up, and kneeled beside the door, red-faced, breathing heavily. "Edie, the Lord said, if we spare the rod, we spoil the child. You've spoiled our child, Edie. And I have spoiled you."

Reynold bent over the crib, turned the baby over onto her stomach, and beat her with an open hand, raising his arm high in the air, thrusting it down again and again across the baby's back and head. He lifted her out and dropped her on the floor outside the room. Then he tossed the crib aside and slammed the door.

He unbelted his jeans and pulled off his shirt, and was soon stripped down to his underwear, the sacred temple garment, a white one-piece jumper. Then he turned Eden onto her back, straddled her body, and hit her repeatedly with his fist.

Eden cried quietly, but did not defend herself, as Reynold pulled off her dress and her temple undergarment, turned her onto her stomach, and lay on top of her, thrusting and grunting.

When he was finished, he lay beside her and held her so tightly that she could scarcely breathe. Small streaks and drops of her blood stained the quilt.

"You'll stay with me tonight," Reynold said. "That's what pleases the Lord. The baby can cry. Crying will be good for her. Crying never killed anyone." He lay for a long time, and breathed short, hot breaths on the back of Eden's head until the moisture condensed in her hair.

Eden lay quiet and still and waited for Reynold to fall asleep. The night had fallen dark and moonless, and a steady wind continued to blow outside that lulled him to sleep. Soon his grip began to loosen and his breaths came slow and deep.

Eden lifted his arm off her naked body, dropped it behind her and tried not to move too abruptly. She winced when she felt his skin rub against her own and fought a shudder when she inadvertently touched his naked thigh. When she finally stood beside the bed, she looked down at the shadowy figure of her husband. Her eyebrows sank low. A contemptuous curl of her lip replaced her submissive frown.

She took her dress from where it lay in the corner, then left the bedroom and closed the door. She pulled a string to turn on the light. The baby lay sleeping, shivering. Her back, neck, and head were bruised from Reynold's beating.

Eden carefully gathered her up and covered her with a thick layer of blankets on the little sofa. In the bathroom, she examined her face. Her left eye was swelling and the left side of her face was red and purple. With a wet hand towel she wiped the drying blood that had trickled from her nose. Then she sat beside the sleeping baby on the sofa and opened a volume of scripture, the New Testament, and began reading.

After an hour the baby awoke and cried out in pain. Eden swaddled and nursed her, whispered lovingly, examined the bruises, spoke in comforting tones. "It'd be better for him to have a millstone tied to his neck and thrown into the sea. Jesus said so. Right into the sea. Should we find us a millstone?" She cast her eyes about the room, detached from her own pain. She stared toward the bedroom for a long time, until she fell asleep.

The wind had picked up, and now whipped at the dead wood of the house in unsteady blasts that whistled through tiny cracks in the window-frames, and around the door. Its cries on the roof's shingles, around the walls, and in the desert brush, sounded like tortured souls.

The sun rose over the east mountains and lit the desert with yellow-orange light, but only briefly. The winds had brought a storm from the west that moved overhead and now covered the last bit of blue in the east and changed the bright morning back to pre-dawn gray. Thunder rumbled far away.

Once the clouds covered the sky, the wind died down, and all was quiet except for the gentle push of a lingering breeze that kept the clouds moving. The crickets and birds and all of nature around the house were quiet.

"Get up, Edie-doll." Reynold caressed Eden's shoulder and ran his fingers through her dark hair, then down her shoulder and across her breast. "Time to wake up, Edie-doll."

Eden's eyes were closed and her face was cradled in her arm. When she raised her head, Reynold saw what he had done, and his eyes grew large.

He turned his face to the floor, trembled, swallowed, then looked again at Eden and tried to look happy. "It's time for breakfast," he said. He leaned down and kissed her on the forehead. Then he kneeled in front of her, took her hand, and seemed like a child talking to an angry parent.

"Wasn't it nice to have a night just for us?" he said. "To hold each other? To fall asleep in each other's arms?"

Eden pulled her hand away from him, disgusted by his touch, and she leaned over to check on the baby.

"Edie, I...I'm afraid I've—"

"No!" Eden raised her small fist. "You don't say nothing now. Not a word."

Reynold watched Eden examine the sleeping baby. And as he watched, his shame faded. He paced in front of the couch making exaggerated gestures with his hands. "Last night I was reading about Adam and Eve. It was what we learn in the temple about obedience, and sacrifice. You see Edie, when you obey my will as I obey God's will, everything becomes holy—you and I become holy. But we can only become holy if you obey the holy order of things. Do you know that? That you must obey me?"

Eden showed no emotion.

"Good," Reynold said. "Obedience, the first law of heaven. That's the first law, Edie. It comes before everything. But what of sacrifice? I look around me and I see no sacrifice from you. I need sacrifice. And God requires it."

Eden tucked the blankets around the baby. "I'll make breakfast."

She turned on the electric stove and placed the pan on the burner, then she unwrapped a slab of bacon and cut six thick slices, lined them side by side in the pan, and watched them sizzle and shrink as they released their grease. She glanced at the small basket beside the stove where four brown eggs lay.

Reynold smiled, satisfied, and went into the bedroom to get dressed. "Smells good, Edie. Smells real good." He stepped out of the bedroom and into the tiny bathroom. "The Lord is about to rain his blessings down on us. I know it. Did you know I worked forty-five hours this week? We'll be out of this old place soon."

After Reynold finished in the bathroom he sat at the table and gazed at Eden as she scooped the bacon slices onto the plate with a fork and poured the bacon fat into a jar near the sink. She broke the eggs into the same pan and mixed them with a wood spoon.

Reynold took a bite of bacon. "You know, Edie, I don't like having to discipline you. It's not something I ever want to do. But I've got to discipline you. That's how it has to be. It's my duty. You know that, right?" His eyes watered and he bit his trembling lip.

Eden stopped stirring the eggs and turned her head just enough to watch Reynold through the corner of her swollen eye.

"I understand what must be done," Eden said.

The eggs popped in the pan and she turned back to the stove to stir them.

Reynold wiped his eyes and nose with his hand. "Okay. Good. We have to be on the same page. We've got to be one flesh. That's what eternity is about, you know, both of us on the same page, forever. A little pain today will bring us eternal blessings. My father used to tell my mother..." He stared at the table. Then he picked up the slice of bacon again and nibbled at it.

Outside, the gray morning began to release some of its rain, and the pattering of large drops struck the roof. Soon, myriad raindrops blended together and became a white noise that made the rest of the world seem silent.

Reynold finished the first slice of bacon and held a second slice between his fingers. "Good thing it's Saturday and no work. Maybe we can have another special night. What do you think, Edie? Like last night?"

"Sure, we can," Eden said. She stepped to the table and scooped the eggs onto the plate, beside the pile of bacon. She turned off the stove and set the pan back on the burner. The bits of eggs in the pan continued to cook. The smoke and its scent rose into the house as the burner slowly cooled from red to black.

Reynold hunched over his plate and savored the bacon, looking up every few seconds like a wild animal protecting a carcass. "What we need to figure out, Edie, is why you have such a rebellious spirit. Just look at this place, this mess. And the baby's crying all the time, and you doing nothing about it.

What we need from you is discipline, Edie. You must have *discipline*. I'm out there working all day, and I come home to a crying baby and burned food and a messy house. That's not discipline. Here's what we'll do from now on..."

While Reynold ate and talked, Eden kneeled beside the sofa and watched the baby sleep. Her body trembled with rage. She cut him off. "What if I leave?"

"You can't leave."

"What if I take the baby, and leave." She saw herself in the small mirror across the room and stared at her beaten face.

"I'm your husband," Reynold said. "I'm God's authority in this home. I am God in this home, Edie, and I say that you can't leave!"

She touched her eyelid, and in the mirror watched her finger press down on the purple skin. "What would you do?"

"Well...well, Edie, I would be forced to show you the mercy that God showed the people in the days of Noah. I would have to apply the penalties for your broken temple covenants. That's God's mercy. That's the way it has to be."

"You would kill me."

"I would."

"We'd hide."

"I would find you."

"You'd be a murderer."

"I would save you for eternity."

"What if you've broke covenants, Rey. What if you're the one that needs punishment, and not me?"

Reynold struck the table with his fists, and the dishes bounced chaotically. "You're talking out of line now, Edie. You're speaking words from Satan's very own mouth. What you're saying is straight from the father of lies."

Eden took a step backward. "You'll never find us."

Reynold pushed his chair back and stood up. His muscles tensed, his blue pupils floated in the round whites of his eyes. "If you break your covenants, Edie, it is my responsibility to be the Lord's hand of vengeance. Do you understand that? I will kill you." After a pause, he added, "To save you from perdition."

"I'm already in perdition, Rey. This is perdition."

Reynold walked around the table, bent down close to Eden's face, and with his jaw rigid, he whispered, "God will not be mocked."

"Pretending to speak for God is mockery," Eden said. She flinched and looked away, expecting another blow to her face.

Reynold turned and sat back at the table to eat his bacon and eggs. "I'll deal with you after breakfast. Go into the bedroom and wait for me there."

Eden did not move.

"Go!"

Eden went into the bedroom and closed the door behind her. Her breath had quickened and she scanned the room. The small bed, the blood-stained quilt, the broken crib turned up on its side, the window. A wood chair sat in the corner and Reynold's tool belt was draped over the back of it. A framing hammer hung down from a leather loop, and its wood handle touched the floor.

She slid the hammer from the loop and held it close to her face, observed the metal, touched it, felt its coolness on her fingertips, and its heaviness in her hands. She raised it above her head and swung.

Then she listened. She no longer heard Reynold's fork on the plate or the smacking of his lips. She moved her hands farther down the handle and took a second, third and fourth practice swing, each time with more confidence than the one before it.

Then in the other room she heard Reynold's chair slide on the floor when he stood up. His bare feet made the floorboards pop and squeak as he approached the bedroom. Soon, he was just outside the bedroom door.

"Edie."

Eden pressed her shoulder against the wall beside the door and raised the hammer over her head. The doorknob wobbled and turned. She held her breath waiting, and watched his hand come into view, then his wrist and forearm. At the first sight of his face, she swung.

The blow glanced off Reynold's forehead and peeled a thin line of skin and hair from above his hairline down to his left eyelid. He staggered backward, and fell, jostled to get on his hands and knees, then crawled frantically toward the kitchen table.

But Eden hovered over him and struck again and again, leaving him little time to move as he covered his head with his hands.

Neither Eden nor Reynold uttered a sound. Their hands, knees and feet scuffled on the floor past the sofa where the baby lay. And with each strike of the hammer the steel struck bone or flesh. Reynold reached the table and gripped the edge of it with his hand. Eden raised the hammer one last time, high above her head, for a final strike.

The blow came down with a crack as the hammer's claws punched through Reynolds skull and sank into the soft matter beneath it. Eden let go, backed away toward the sofa, and watched.

Reynold froze for a few seconds before his arms and legs buckled beneath him and he toppled over sideways. The hammer dislodged from his skull and slid across the wood floor.

His mouth gaped wide, as if a wedge had been forced into his jaw. His hands were pulled up to his chest, and his fingers flexed into loose fists, quaking. His eyes widened as he stared up at Eden. Beneath his head, a pool of blood expanded, and soon his head was framed in deep red.

In a few minutes, his arms and legs relaxed. The pool of blood stopped expanding. His mouth and eyes remained open and still.

The baby continued to sleep only a few feet away on the little sofa under the thick cover of blankets. Outside, the rain fell harder and turned the dirt road and the desert into vast pools of sticky clay, dotted with brush.

Ω

Carolyn sat on her porch and smelled the sweet and bitter odors that the desert offered during rainfalls. She held her hand out from under the awning to feel the summer raindrops on her skin. In the yard, in the vacant lots and quiet construction sites, and in all the fields, the clay earth failed to soak up water as quickly as the water came, and large pools formed everywhere.

Across the field, Carolyn saw the shack's door open. Eden stepped into the mud wearing her old yellow dress that hung loose on her willow-like body, and work boots that seemed much too large. She retrieved a shovel that leaned against the wall and walked a dozen yards into the brush, fighting against the mud with each step. Then she began to dig.

Carolyn watched, bemused, until her ten-year-old daughter called from inside.

"Mom!"

"What do you need, sweetie?"

Her daughter opened the door, wide-eyed. She held a wet rag in her hand. "Davie soiled his diaper." She left the door open and ran around the corner, into the kitchen.

Before Carolyn went inside, she glanced once more through the rain, toward the shack, where Eden continued to dig.

Around noon Carolyn returned to the porch. The rain had calmed, but a light sprinkle seemed to float in the air, and the clouds hung lower in the sky. Across the field Eden now stood thigh-deep in a hole. Her dress was soaked and covered in mud, and the fabric stuck to her body from the neck down, revealing her gaunt features more plainly. Her dark hair straddled her shoulders in strings.

She had built up a semicircular hill of dirt and mud just outside the hole. But her work had slowed, and she raised the shovelfuls of water-logged soil, lifted it to ground level, slid the spade up the small hill, turned the shovel over, then dragged it back down.

Carolyn watched for a few minutes, then went back into the house. In the small master bedroom, she put on an old dress and a pair of boots. Then she went back through the living room, toward the front door.

"Where you going?" her daughter asked, "Are you all right, mama?"

"I'm checking on the neighbors. Everything's all right."

"Can I come?"

"I need you to watch your brothers till I get back. I might be a while."

The children watched from the porch as their mother walked away.

Carolyn clomped through the mud and through the shallow pools of brown water. Her boots sank into the wet clay with each step and made a sucking sound when she pulled them out of the mud again. She crossed the yard, walked more easily along the gravel road, then turned onto the dirt road that led to Eden's house. Several times, when the caked clay became too heavy on her boots, she gouged into it with her fingers to scoop away as much as she could. Finally, out of breath and soaked by the steady rain, she arrived at the rectangular hole Eden was digging.

"Eden, are you okay?"

Eden turned a shovelful of mud onto the pile and looked up from the hole. Her face was splashed with clay, and her hair was matted with it, her yellow dress was now soaked and browned. Drops of rain mingled with her sweat and dripped down her face and fell off her chin. She wiped her forehead with a dirty sleeve and said, "What are you doing here?" Then she dragged the shovel back into the hole and pushed it into the wet dirt.

Carolyn observed Eden's swollen and bruised cheeks and the black eye and knew Reynold had done it but was unable to decide what to do or what to say. For several minutes, she only watched.

Eden worked methodically, digging out one side of the rectangular hole at a time, alternating sides often. On and on she whittled away the inches, frequently using a boot to push heavy layers of wet clay off the shovel. Her thin arms and legs trembled from hours of labor.

The rain began to pick up again, and the sound of countless more raindrops slapping the wet ground seemed to intensify Eden's efforts.

Carolyn shouted through the rain. "Eden, for goodness sake, what are you doing?"

"I'm digging a hole."

Carolyn wiped water from her eyes and forehead with the back of her hand. "But why? Where's your husband?"

"He's inside."

"Where's your baby?"

"She's in there, too." Eden switched sides, pushed mud off the shovel with her boot, then resumed digging.

Carolyn stepped closer. "What's this about?"

Eden pushed the shovel into the bottom of the hole so that it remained upright. Then she reached out, gripped the branches of a rabbit brush and pulled herself out, crawling, dragging her dress through the mud. She faced Carolyn and examined her features with her strange eyes. "We don't know each other."

"No, Eden, we don't, but—"

"Go look inside. But don't wake the baby."

Carolyn turned to the house, trudged to the doorstep and looked back. Eden had not moved, but watched, still and silent.

She cracked the door open and peered inside. She could see the baby sleeping under several layers of blankets on the old sofa. There was the lingering scent of bacon and eggs, and another odd smell, metallic and sweet, as when a fresh-killed pig is strung up and blood streams from its cut throat.

She pushed the door wide open and saw Reynold lying on the floor. He lay on his side with his knees bent and pulled up to his chest. His mouth was open, contorted, as if about to scream, and his dry, glazed-over eyes seemed to stare at her. A pool of coagulating blood had spread out from his head on the wood floor.

Carolyn backed against the doorframe and covered her mouth firmly with both hands to keep from screaming. Her stomach began to heave as if to vomit. She averted her eyes from the body, but soon looked at it again. Tears began to form, but did not fall. To calm herself, she tried to breathe more deeply. Soon she turned to the baby, hoping to find her alive, merely sleeping.

She moved to the sofa with her back against the wall to where the baby lay and found she was sleeping, sweating and red-faced under the cover of several blankets. She had been holding back tears, but now she let them fall, and she breathed a deep shuddering sigh, then carefully pulled away the covers.

Carolyn winced when she saw the purple and black skin on the back and side of the baby's head. She knew Reynold had beat both Eden and the baby. A wave of disgust passed through her.

She tucked a thin blanket around the baby's cheeks and left the other blankets on the floor, then turned to the dead body.

The strip of skin hung beside his eye. Portions of his hair were matted with dried blood. A hammer lay on the floor a few feet away.

When Carolyn stepped back outside, Eden still stood beside the hole watching for her reaction. For a minute, the women observed each other silently.

"You see what the hole's for?" Eden asked.

"You killed him!"

"I did what I had to do."

"We need to call the police," said Carolyn.

"I'm not calling them. I'm digging a grave. I killed him, and I'm not going to jail for doing it."

"Look, I've heard him yelling, Eden. I know he beat you and the baby. You've got the bruises. You were only protecting yourself. We have to call the police!"

Eden slid back into the hole. A hint of indignation crossed her brow when she took the shovel in her hands. "I wasn't protecting myself. When I stuck that hammer in his head he
was crawling on the floor like a baby, trying to get away. I didn't have to do it. I wasn't fighting him off. I wanted to do it. It was God's will. But the law, the police, they don't know God's will. They'd figure it out, and they'd put me away."

"But you'll go to jail if you don't call the police and they find out—"

The sky burned white for an instant, and both women instinctively raised their arms to cover their faces. A second later the thunder exploded.

Eden lowered her arm after the rumble faded. "Listen, I don't have time to argue. You go ahead and tell the police if you want. I'm gonna keep on doing what I'm doing."

A gust of wind, a colder wind from the north, blew in and chilled their wet clothes.

"There's more storm coming," Carolyn cried. "A bigger one!" She faced the wind and saw the darker clouds moving fast toward Fillmore.

"Then go on home," Eden said. "Just go home and forget all this."

"If I go home...if the police ever find out I knew...I'll be thrown in jail, too."

"I'd never tell nobody you was here."

Carolyn looked homeward, brushed a wet strand of hair from her face, and looked down at her hands to watch the raindrops make little clean dots on her skin. She could call the police and Eden may go to prison. Or she could help make sure Reynold's body was buried quickly, and nobody would ever know. She thought of a verse from Mormon scripture, which teaches *it is better for one man to die than for many to perish in unbelief.* Perhaps Reynold is the *one man.* Maybe this was God's will...

"Okay, Eden," said Carolyn, "we've got to get this done faster, before my husband comes home, before anyone sees us out here like this." She kneeled in the mud and held out her hand. "Let me take a turn. You're worn out."

Eden observed Carolyn suspiciously, but then her face softened. "I guess it's about time to bring him out here." She took Carolyn's hand and climbed out.

Carolyn slipped into the hole and took the shovel. "Make sure to put something under his head if you're going to move him. Don't drag blood everywhere."

Eden nodded and went inside.

Carolyn raised the mud-filled shovel again and again, turned it onto the pile, then pulled the shovel back into the hole.

The rain intensified.

Inside the house, Eden lifted Reynold's shoulders and turned him over onto his back. His stiffening muscles made his limbs settle slowly into their new positions.

She brought a muddy piece of plywood in from outside and laid it beside him, then lifted his shoulders and scooted him onto it.

His face, still contorted as if to make a death cry, and his eyes horrified and fearful, now made Eden shudder in disgust. She pulled an old bedsheet from the nails in the bedroom window and wrapped his head and upper body in it and drew two corners under his arms and tied them in a knot across his chest so it would not slip off. Then she took his ankles, pivoted him around, and dragged him on the sheet of plywood across the floor.

All this was done, and the baby did not stir.

Carolyn worked for thirty minutes and made good progress. She stood chest deep in the hole. When she saw Eden struggle to pull the body through the mud, and tried to climb out, the heaviness of her wet dress and her boots weighed her legs down. She reached for the strong branches of the rabbit brush and pulled herself out, sliding on her stomach, until she could get her knees under her. Then she slogged toward the doorstep, where Eden had dragged Reynold's body. Each woman took an ankle, and they slid the body between piles of wood and scrap metal, over the yellow wheat grass, and into the hole. The body was longer than the hole, and the feet and the hems of his jeans almost stuck out into the open.

Eden climbed in and stepped around the body in the mud, and pulled Reynold's upper half until his neck was bent against one side of the pit. Then she straddled him with one foot at his shoulder and another near his hips, and she bent his legs so that he was curled up in a fetal position.

Carolyn helped her climb out.

They looked down at the jeans, the bare feet, the muddy white undershirt, the head and shoulders wrapped in the sheet. Large raindrops continued, and water dripped from the ends of their soaked hair, fell on their skin and on their sodden dresses, and began to wash the slippery mud in streaks that revealed the colors beneath.

Eden held out her hands. They were covered with mud and blood, and she watched, trancelike, as points of clean skin appeared on her palms. But soon her sense of urgency returned and she took the shovel by the handle. "I got to get this hole filled," she said. Then she pulled the spade out of the mud. "You got to go home to your kids, and I got to finish up."

"What are we going to do?" Carolyn asked.

Eden turned her back to Carolyn and held the shovel in both hands. "You don't need to do nothing. You helped, and I thank you. I'll finish up here. You go home and forget all this. Just forget."

The lightning and thunder had passed over to the mountains, and it flashed and sounded in the distance, muffled by the shushing drone of the rain.

"How could I forget this?" Carolyn said. "Somebody's going to find out about it. It won't stay secret."

"I told you to go ahead and call the police," Eden said. "You do what you got to do. I done what I had to do. But whatever you do, do it quickly. There's no sense waiting."

Eden gripped the shovel like a canoe paddle and began to scoop the pile of dirt back into the hole. She did not look up or stop her work while she spoke. "You better get going. Your kids are probably wondering where you're at and what you're doing over here. Let's pray they seen nothing."

"I'll come over tomorrow, or the next day, after the ground dries up a little."

Eden did not respond.

As Carolyn walked home through the deep slippery clay and through the brown pools of water, she stopped every so often to look back, to see Eden filling the hole. Each time, the pile of mud beside the grave was a little smaller.

When she finally climbed the steps to her porch, exhausted, ragged-looking, and soaked through and through, she fell to her knees and clasped her hands together. Then she bowed her head and cried, "Heavenly Father!"

Ω

Bishop Argyle had not shifted in his chair or averted his eyes as he listened to Eden's tale. She had given a brief version, short on details. He now knew that she once had an abusive and perhaps insane husband, she killed him one morning with a hammer and buried him in a shallow grave with the help of a dear friend.

Both were quiet for a while after she finished, each of them pondering what should come next.

But soon, Eden's face became resolute and she pointed a finger at the bishop. "I killed him. Not because he hurt us, but because it was God's will. I chased him down with that hammer and I stuck it in his head, and I watched him die. And I never once thought it was a sin. That was a sacred moment, a holy one."

"I don't know what to say, Sister Lebaron." Bishop Argyle glanced at the manual for Bishops that he had pushed aside earlier. "I think we have to call the police."

"You go ahead and do whatever you need to do, Evan."

Bishop Argyle rubbed his forehead with his hand, then he ran his index finger along the wood grain on his desk. "You said someone helped you that day?"

"Yes, a very kind neighbor helped out. She trodged in the mud and worked at digging and helped me get him in the hole. She and I become dear friends after that. And just like you, she said we ought to call the police."

Bishop Argyle examined the wrinkles on Eden's skin. "I remember calling you Grandma Eden when I was growing up. You've always been Grandma Eden."

"And I always loved being one of your grandmas, Evan."

"And you and Grandma Argyle were constantly together at your place or at her place, especially after grandpa died."

"We was best friends."

Bishop Argyle closed his eyes. When he opened them, tears were forming. "Your friend...the friend that helped you...when did she die?"

"Evan, we both know the answer to that question. Your grandmother, Carolyn, passed away about ten years ago."

Bishop Argyle turned his gaze back to the wood grain on his desk. His eyes watered, and his breath was uneven as he held his emotions. "We need to call somebody about this."

"You know, you and her are the same kind of good. Far as I know, she lived and died thinking she should've called the police. But she could never do it. She never quite knew what was the right thing to do."

"This is a very serious sin, Sister Lebaron. A crime. This isn't something I can overlook. You don't kill people. You turn them in. You get away from them. You defend yourself if they're attacking you. But you don't kill them for justice or for vengeance. You don't play God."

"Evan, do you believe sometimes it's necessary for one man to die so that many people don't perish? It's in the *Book of Mormon*, you know, with Nephi and Laban, and with Nehor. When the Holy Ghost prompts—"

"Sister Lebaron, this has nothing to do with that."

"I think it has very much to do with that," Eden said. "Is this about the temple covenants? Because he wasn't—"

"This is about so much more than that! This is about a family that never knew what happened to their son. This is about human decency. It's about your daughter never knowing what happened to her father. It's so much more than the temple."

"I understand, Evan. I do understand what you think. Just decide what you're gonna do and do it quickly." Eden's eyes were like a wind-tossed sea. "Evan, all that's important is we get the records straight in heaven and on earth. I knew I'd have to tell a priesthood leader about this eventually and get things all cleared up. But I knew nobody would understand. So, I waited. I've been faithful, always faithful to the church. That's why I held out till now…so I could live a life. You understand? God had much for me to accomplish, so I didn't say nothing. But now I'm old, the record's got to be straight."

Just then, there was a light knock on the door, and the rumpled Executive Secretary opened it just enough to reveal his face and his unkempt hair. "I canceled your appointments until four o'clock."

"Oh. Okay. Thank you, Brother Morgan."

After the door was shut, the bishop leaned forward and cradled his forehead in his hand. He watched Eden reach into her set of scriptures and pull out a tiny slip of paper. It was her temple recommend; a document required for admission into the temple.

"I think you'll need this," Eden said. "I always thought I needed this. But I know you have to take it away from me. A killer shouldn't be a temple worker." She placed the temple recommend on the table and pushed it toward him.

Bishop Argyle took the piece of paper and studied it. He remembered signing it, and now he examined the signature, a string of scribbles. His thoughts raced.

"Evan, when I tell you to figure out what you're gonna do, and to do it quickly, I mean it," Eden said. "If the police show up to get me, I'd rather it be sooner than later."

She saw the bishop's distress, shook her head, and laughed, "You're just like your grandmother. I could see it all the way back when you was born. Such a sweet boy. A sweet man. But you don't know how to make decisions when two sins oppose each other." She took up her heavy book in one arm and used her free hand to push herself up off the chair. "I've said all that I come to say. You know my sin now, if you call it a sin. You're the judge in Israel here, and you write heaven's book. So, I'll go now and let you write it." She turned to the door and said, "Evan, I'll endure whatever punishment you see fit for me."

Bishop Argyle did not stand up to shake her hand, as he was accustomed to doing. His face was white. His fingers trembled lightly as he pulled the manual back in front of him. He did not look up when Eden walked out.

When the door clicked shut, Bishop Argyle pushed his chair away from the desk and kneeled on the floor. With his hands clasped together, with his head bowed, he prayed.

Many Sparrows

The sun shone pleasantly in Rio's partly cloudy sky, bathing in warm light the tourists on the beaches of the Guanabara Bay, the gated communities, the busy highways, the people who walked to work, to school, or to wherever life was leading them under the blue sky. High in the hills, Jesus seemed to watch with outstretched hands.

In Rio's largest slum, in its narrow, disorganized alleys, the sky was often hidden by the endless maze of high brick and plaster walls and corrugated metal eaves. The cement paths were gray, the tin was gray, and even the colorfully painted plaster took an ashen tint. Add the smell of so many people living in such a small area, fresh, putrid, sweet, bitter, and all the sounds, loud, soft, tender, violent. The combined effect was oppression.

Little barefoot boys in tank tops and shorts played soccer, shouting, laughing, cheering. Juvenile boys, who sat silently in nooks and dark corners, held plastic bags over their mouths and noses, and breathed the fumes of the rubber cement they had scavenged. Women and girls, chatting, washed clothes on cement washboards. Men wandered around as if they had somewhere to go, their faces angry, scared, deadpan.

Two young men, Mormon missionaries, passed the morning hours and most of the afternoon on the slum's narrow cement paths and little courtyards. They stopped at every door, tapped, then offered their message to whoever answered. Then they smiled politely when rejected, again and again and again. The people of the slum did not have patience for nonsense.

The missionaries were set apart from everyone else by their white short-sleeved shirts, dark ties, and dark slacks. Black name tags were clipped to their breast pockets. No older than twenty, they walked like men but looked like boys. With their Jansport book bags tossed over a shoulder, they could have been mistaken for university students.

After five hours of door-to-door rejection, their eyes had a far-away stare and their gaits had slowed. Their brief discussions with faces at the doors became monotonous, mechanical.

Humidity made the day seem warmer than it really was, and the underarms of their shirts were darkened with sweat.

They stopped at a tiny corner-store where the alley widened into a kind of courtyard, and each missionary purchased a bottle of Coca-Cola. Then they sat on the cement, in the shade, and sipped their drinks.

The taller of the two missionaries was not well. His short, curly, dark hair was disheveled from running his hands through it too often. With two fingers, he compulsively rubbed a spot high on his forehead near his hair line, and a red rash, swollen and cracked, had formed there. He mumbled something about shadows, but his sentences and phrases were jumbled and incomplete. The name printed on his nametag was *Elder Demas*. Back in Utah his name was Matthew.

Matthew gulped down his drink so that the liquid sloshed on his face and dripped onto his shirt and made light brown stains. His eyes darted right and left, vigilant, nervous, terrified. And aside from aggravating the sore on his forehead, he sometimes covered his ears or his eyes, or he scruffed his hair with both hands as if it were infested with spiders.

After finishing his drink, Matthew suddenly looked into the alley. "They're coming now."

Elder Sousa, whose name was Gabriel back at home in Sao Paulo, laid his empty Coke bottle on the cement. Then he turned away from Matthew and closed his eyes. He prayed silently about what to do. He should have called mission leaders weeks ago when he first knew that Matthew's hallucinations did not come from sleep deprivation, or from long days in the sun, or from door after door of rejection. He should—

"What are you doing?" Matthew cried.

"Nothing. Give me a moment." Gabriel said. Today he would call President Olivares, the mission president. That was the only possible answer to his prayer.

"You're angry."

Gabriel turned around. "I'm not angry, Elder. I'm worried about you. What do you see right now, when you look there in the path?"

"The shadows," Matthew said. "And they're already here. They came from there and from there, in rows. And now one of them stands at each door, and two stand at those stairs over there."

"They're the same shadows you saw at the apartment and at church?"

"Yes."

"What are they doing, aside from standing there?"

"They're just staring at us. They're standing straight like soldiers, but they're looking at me. They're saying things."

"What are they saying?"

"Too much to hear. They're all talking at once. I can't understand. It's like…it's like they're chanting, all at different times, to confuse." Matthew gestured exaggeratedly with his hands, and his voice varied from low to high when he spoke. He hunched his back and continued to rub the same place on his forehead, which had begun to bleed through tiny cracks in the skin. "I can't understand them."

"Let's go home and rest awhile," Gabriel said.

"Look around! Where can we go?"

"It will be okay, Elder Demas. This isn't—"

Matthew leaped to his feet and backed against the wall. "You stay away from me." He aimed a fist at Gabriel. His eyes watered, his face twisted with fear.

Just then, a soccer ball bounced off the wall and rolled downhill toward the missionaries. A small boy chased the ball, picked it up and held it at his side, then watched the missionaries with big curious eyes. Soon, he ran back to the corner and summoned the other children with an enthusiastic gesture. A half-dozen children soon watched and whispered to each other about the strange, overdressed men.

Matthew's eyes widened. "Elder Sousa! Don't you see all of them? There are so many. How can we go anywhere? How can we get home? How can we even move?"

Gabriel took Matthew by the arm. "Let's go."

Matthew pulled away and glared.

"Be calm, Elder. Be calm," Gabriel said. He touched Matthew on the shoulder. "It's okay, Elder Demas. You're safe. Let's go home. Okay?"

With a violent shove Matthew flung Gabriel into a cinderblock wall. Gabriel slid to the ground and held the back of his head. His face twisted with the pain.

"You're not Elder Sousa!"

The children shrieked with delight to see Matthew's outburst, and some of them ran to call more friends. A few doors opened just wide enough for men and women to see what was going on.

Gabriel stumbled to his feet and leaned against the wall. He blinked a few times and looked up at the sky until his sight became more focused. His arms dropped to his sides and his hands knotted into tight fists.

"Elder Demas," Gabriel said, "I don't want to hurt you, but you need to listen to me. We're going home!"

Matthew was fixated on something to his left and whispered incoherently about it. But then he turned again to Gabriel, "You're not Elder Sousa!" And he swung his fists.

Gabriel threw his right fist and crushed Matthew's nose. Matthew staggered backward and struck a light pole. Blood flowed from his nose, rolled over his lips and dripped from his chin onto his shirt. In a rage he struck back, swinging wildly. But Gabriel bent down low, fired out, and plunged his shoulder into Matthew's stomach. Their flailing limbs thumped against the cement when they fell, and Matthew's head struck with a hollow pop. Gabriel straddled Matthew's chest and swung at his face until Matthew stopped struggling.

Out of breath, Gabriel rolled onto his back on the cement and stared at the sky. His eyes welled with tears and he turned his head to Matthew. "Forgive me, Elder Demas. Please forgive me."

Matthew groaned and tried to sit up, but he was disoriented. He touched his face and mingled his fingers in the blood that flowed from his nose and dripped down his cheeks to the cement. "I'm sorry too."

By now a crowd of men, women and children filled the alley, and they whispered their astonishment one to another. The children, convinced the excitement was over, retreated to their games.

Gabriel sat up, took off his tie and rolled it up, then held it to Matthew's nose. When Matthew took hold of the tie, Gabriel picked up Matthew's book bag and laid it beside his own, then stretched out his hand. "Can you get up?"

Matthew took Gabriel's hand, and soon he leaned against the wall. Gabriel slung both their backpacks onto one shoulder then put his other arm around Matthew. Then the crowd parted spontaneously to let them through, and the missionaries quietly navigated the narrow paths to their apartment.

The apartment consisted of a single room just large enough for two twin beds, and an open bathroom consisting of a toilet and shower, partitioned from the rest of the room with a thick plastic curtain. The room seemed more like a jail cell than an apartment.

Gabriel dropped the backpacks on the floor and helped Matthew to lie down. Then he sat on his bed with his elbows on his knees and closed his eyes. He prayed in silence for a long time and listened to Matthew's breathing as it became more relaxed. The next time Gabriel looked up, Matthew's nose had stopped bleeding. His face was covered with dried and drying blood. Matthew was awake, staring at the ceiling.

"Elder Demas," Gabriel said. "You're not getting better. You're getting worse. We need to call for help."

Tears rolled down Matthew's cheeks. "I — I think you're right."

"I'm going to call President Oliveira now, okay?"

"Wait," Matthew said. "When you call the President, I'll be sent home. We know this. My mission will be over." He wiped his cheeks with his palms, smearing the tears and the blood. "Do you think you could give me a blessing before you call?"

Gabriel hesitated, and opened his mouth as if to say something, then bit his lower lip and nodded. Matthew clasped his hands together on his chest and closed his eyes as Gabriel stepped to his bedside and laid his hands on Matthew's head.

There was a long moment of silence while Gabriel prepared himself for the blessing.

"Matthew Lehi Demas," Gabriel began, "by the authority of the Holy Melchizedek Priesthood, I lay my hands on your head to give you a blessing..." Gabriel went on, and said whatever thoughts came to mind. He spoke optimistically about Matthew's future and counseled him to seek the help he needed. He reminded him that he was a child of God.

When the blessing was over, Matthew took Gabriel's hand and thanked him. Then Gabriel dialed the Mission President.

A week later, Matthew was on an airplane to the Salt Lake City International Airport. His mother waited alone for his flight to arrive.

Ω

The judge sat at his elevated bench and scowled down at a small packet of stapled pages. After every few breaths, he flipped to the next page, held the corner while he read, and then flipped to the next. After several minutes, and having reviewed every page, he looked up.

He was a straight-faced, stern-looking man, and he glared down at Kristi Burton, who sat at the defendant's table. The social workers and guardian ad litem had said their piece, and the judge was required to act accordingly and give Kristi custody of her daughter.

But he had to get some things off his chest first.

"Your child is seven years old," he said. Then he paused for an uncomfortable amount of time and flipped again through the paperwork he was about to sign. "You've disrupted her life more than any adult could ever bear. Could you bear it? Could you live with your shenanigans if you were her? Don't answer. Of course, you couldn't. None of us could."

The judge gestured to Kristi's parents. "These people, for better or worse, they have saved your life. We've all been here before, watched you act teary-eyed and contrite, this whole show. Let me tell you...there's nothing good or noble about what we're going to do right now. But I must do what the law requires, and right now I'm required to give your daughter back to you, like sending a lamb to the slaughter. Let me tell you this much, I don't ever want to see you again. In these small towns, I'm the only judge you'll ever get, and we're both sick of seeing each other. Do you understand? Don't answer that. Of course, you don't understand."

He rested an elbow on his desk and tossed open the document to the last page, where his signature was required. He set the tip of his pen on the signature line, paused, then put the pen down and gave Kristi an angry glare.

"Our system doesn't protect children," the judge said. "It protects you. Our laws don't care about these kids. You are the one who will destroy her life, and you are the one who can save it. Frankly, I have no confidence in you. My only comfort is that we're requiring you to live with your parents. And that's little comfort."

The judge then turned to Kristi's parents, David and Susan Burton. "You two created this, and you've facilitated the addictions. If I could hold you legally responsible for some of this, I would. But as you know, I can't."

Then the judge signed on the designated line.

That evening after dinner, after Kristi's daughter Audrey went to bed, Kristi and her parents stayed in the dining room in the warm glow of the low ambient light. The light conversation about happy things had fizzled, and Kristi glanced at her father, who averted his eyes.

They all knew what was coming next.

Susan flipped on the overhead lights that filled the room with midday brightness. "Let's get started."

David sat up, business-like, opened a folder he had laid on the table earlier in the evening, and retrieved a sheet of paper full of notes. Kristi stared at the table. Susan sat beside David and looked somberly at Kristi.

David's hand trembled a little, and the tremble was amplified in the page he was holding. He coughed and

glanced at Susan, then the words stumbled out. "This is the last chance," he said. "This time it's got to be different, sweetheart. Your mother and me have done a lot of thinking, and we're going to...I mean, what's got to happen is—"

Susan finished the thought. "What's got to happen, Kristi, is you've got to finally grow up. This is your last chance, and our last chance too." She took the notes from David. "We've made a list of rules. And you'll have to abide by them. If you slip, even once, we're finished. We love you dearly. But the judge was right about you and us. Unless you keep these rules, we're cutting you off." When Susan finished, she closed her eyes to keep the tears in. David put his arm around her and kissed her forehead.

Kristi took a deep breath and tried to smile. "I know I'll need your help for a while until I get on my feet. I'll need your rules. I learned some new things in rehab. With addicts, like me, we can never seem to make a right choice. It seems like every choice leads us farther and farther into trouble. And when I look back over the last eight years, since I was sixteen, I see that. I made bad choice after bad choice, always thinking I was choosing the right. I watched some of my friends do the same thing, some of them are dead now. I'll need rules to play by, at least for a while."

David smiled admiringly.

"Okay, Kristi," Susan said. "I appreciate that you recognize the need for this." She looked down again at the page in her hand. "First, you're going to have a curfew. Eleven o'clock is lights out. You'll be in the house, and it's bedtime."

Kristi bit her lower lip. "Okay."

"Second, you're going to work. Enrique over at Lopez Automotive told us he'll hire you. You'll work the counter. Your first day is Monday."

"I've always loved Mr. Lopez," Kristi said.

"I thought you'd like that part of this list," Susan said.

David winked.

"Your rent will be two-hundred-fifty, plus one hundred for utilities, so three-hundred-fifty every month, due on the first..."

Over the next hour Kristi agreed to numerous rules. Certain old friends were off limits. Parenting rules for her daughter, Audrey, were written in detail. Goals were set for the near future. Kristi could use the old Mercedes to get to the weekly twelve-step meetings in Nephi, and to take Audrey to visit her other grandparents in Delta.

"You're twenty-five," Susan said. "But in so many ways you're sixteen. We lost you then, and you lost yourself. Let's get your life back, okay?"

Before Kristi could respond, Audrey entered from the hallway, her eyes half-closed, blinking in the bright light.

"What's happening?" Audrey asked.

"Oh, sweetie, come here," Susan said.

Audrey was always open for a hug for any reason, or for no reason at all, and she wrapped her little arms around her grandparents as far as she could stretch them.

Kristi got up from her seat and embraced them all.

Audrey giggled.

April

The walls of Matthew's room were covered with painted canvasses, and more canvasses leaned in stacks against the wall beside his twin bed. Wildlife and nature scenes from his early years were created in a noticeably more amateur hand compared to the rest. But his later paintings, looking more like a brilliant mad artist's, were more abundant.

Soon after he returned from his mission in Brazil, having come home several months shy of the standard two years, his paintings and sketches had taken an ominous turn, and the figures of his mind were manifested in the art that littered his room. After only a few months his room was stacked with strange paintings.

Matthew stood beside his mother, Stephanie Demas, in his bedroom, and they looked thoughtfully at a canvass that still glistened with wet paint. The easel sat on a sheet of thick plastic that protected the floor. Paints, brushes, a pail of thinner, and a palette were scattered about.

"It's nice," Stephanie said. "But what's it supposed to be?"

"It's the world the way I see it sometimes. I saw something like this in Brazil, and it's always on my mind. Look up close. Tell me what you see."

"Here's what I see," Stephanie said. "That half of the painting looks like a vertical sunset. The red streaks of the sunset look a little like bloodstains, like someone dragged a bleeding animal across the canvass. This other half looks as if it's already night-time. There are people in the darkness, or the shadows of people, and they're staring out at us. I can just see the outlines of their faces and shoulders, and their eyes. Here, right in the middle, in the midst of the red streak, there's a thin stream of light, but it doesn't shine into the darkness." She rubbed the goosebumps on her arm. "But, if I'm not paying attention or looking closely at it, I would probably want it in my living room. It's really that pretty. That's what I see. Is that about right?"

"Well, yeah, that's what the painting is, mom. But it's so much more. This is me. I am this."

Stephanie looked away, and in her worry she clasped her hands together so tightly that her fingertips turned red. "It's very nice."

Matthew turned to work at folding the pile of clean laundry that lay on his bed. "Do you think I can take some food?" he asked.

"Sure," Stephanie said. "And I've got some money to tide you over until next weekend." She took the empty laundry basket and left the room.

Matthew finished folding his clothes and stacked them in a canvas laundry bag. Then he loaded the brushes, paints, palette and the paint thinner into a plastic bin and carried it all outside for a good cleaning.

In a short time, everything was boxed and stored for another week, and Matthew's car was packed with his clothes and a box of food.

He hugged his mother "I love you, mom. Thanks for everything."

"I love you too, Matthew. Please be safe."

"I'll be safe, mom."

Matthew blinked rapidly and rubbed his forehead.

"Are you feeling okay? Did you take your medicine?" Stephanie placed her hand on Matthew's forehead, as if testing his temperature.

"Yeah, I took it. I'm feeling...I'm feeling okay."

"Just okay?"

"Yes. Just okay. And that's good enough. It'll be better once I get this semester over with."

Soon, Matthew drove away.

Ω

Kristi sat on a metal folding chair in a small church classroom normally used for youth Sunday School, but on that night, it was the meeting place for a handful of people attending an addiction recovery support group sponsored by the church. The hum of the air conditioner was barely noticeable, except when it switched on or off. At eight o'clock in the evening, the hot July sun had almost an hour before it fell behind the west hills. Its light shone through the opaque west-facing window.

Six people, including Kristi, sat around the room. An older man and woman who wore their black missionary name tags, sat together holding hands. Aside from the missionaries and Kristi, three men, at varying stages of recovery, were in the room.

One of the men, who looked to be in his early thirties, said, "When I was hooked, I thought I had it all under control, you know? That I could stop at any time. But I knew in my heart of hearts that I was out of control. I always felt ashamed afterward, but in the moment, I never cared, or I found a way to justify myself. I convinced myself that I was fine, that my family was fine, that everything in my life was fine. But that little part of me, buried in there, knew the truth."

He was talking to a younger man, whose eyes were red from crying. The crying man turned to the missionaries. "I think about it constantly. At home, at work. I even masturbate while driving. It's almost like I'm not the person inhabiting my body. It has destroyed my marriage...my life."

The more experienced man put a hand on his shoulder. "I've been there. I'm here for you. I'll be here every Tuesday night."

"You know," Kristi said, "things can and do get better. But you can't give up after the first week. You can't give up after the first month. I'm ten months in, and I'm learning a lot. But I'm still far from being whole. I still want to feed my addiction every single day. I almost relapsed this week. Almost." She blew out a breath. "I know where to find meth or oxy or heroin. I know exactly how much it costs in cash or in favors. I could get it in ten minutes."

"What helps you resist the temptation?" Sister Olsen asked. She was a missionary, a kind-looking grey-haired woman with long, straight hair.

"I don't know, exactly," Kristi said. "My daughter, for one. I've put her through hell—" She stopped abruptly, remembering even the mildest vulgarity was not appropriate among the faithful. "Excuse me," she said. "*Heck*. I've put her through heck."

Sister Olsen, laughed. "There's a good time for a well-placed curse word. Don't apologize when you use a swear word fittingly." Everyone, even the tearful newcomer, laughed to hear a missionary endorse mild vulgarity.

"Okay," Kristi said, "I put my daughter through hell. And my parents too. I think making it right is my motivation. I'm older now, and stronger. I know how my actions have hurt people, and I don't want to hurt the people I love anymore."

"Good," Sister Olsen's husband said. His nametag identified him as Brother Olsen. "What else?"

"I've been praying," Kristi said, "and reading the scriptures. I think that helps—"

"Does it?" The crying man's expression had turned to anger.

Kristi looked to the missionaries.

Sister Olsen said to the man, "Go on."

"I've read the scriptures every day since I was a teenager," the man said. "I've prayed every day. I attend church every week. I've served wherever I've been asked. I love my God, my wife and my children. I try so hard to be good." His tears had stopped by now, and his face had reddened. "I do all of this, and I have not been able to break my addiction. I go back and back and back again, every time, no matter how hard I've tried. Prayer and scriptures, and all the other religious stuff we're told will help, none of it has ever helped me."

"I'm sorry," Kristi said. "I didn't mean to hurt anyone's feelings. I —"

"Why doesn't it work for me!" the man cried. "I feel like God is playing a cruel joke. I feel like his promises are lies."

The two other men nodded their heads. One spoke up. "We know. You pray and plead and read and pray and pray some more, but the next moment, there you are, back at it."

"I'm sorry if I don't understand," Kristi said. "I'm new to church and prayer and scriptures and all this."

Sister Olsen got the conversation back on track. "Thank you, everyone, for the good discussion. I think what we should realize is that everyone is different. From person to person, the approach for fighting addiction, and the length of time, will be different for everyone. There is no simple way, no single answer."

The man wiped his cheeks with the back of his hand. "Then why is prayer, scripture study and church attendance always the go-to recipe for solving every life problem? That's all they say you need to do, and then the Lord is supposed to give you strength to overcome any challenge."

"I think the reason people say that," Sister Olsen said, "is probably because people don't know what else to say. Maybe they can't comprehend that there's no quick fix that works for everybody. They don't understand that the Lord doesn't work the same way with everybody. Have you ever told anyone to solve their problems with church attendance, scriptures and prayer?"

"Yeah," the man said. "When I was younger. When I was a missionary."

Sister Olsen said, "Me too. I said it even when I was older, unfortunately. And I regret it. After meeting so many good people like you, and discovering how inadequate that advice is for addiction, I regret ever having given such a simple, ignorant answer."

The classroom was quiet for a few seconds.

"I've been thinking," Kristi said. "What is the reason we go through this? I'm not talking about just making a bad choice. I know we're free to make choices. But why did God even allow addiction? Did God create addiction?"

"I'd like to know that too," Sister Olsen said. "That's going to be one of my first questions for him when I see him again."

The class continued only a little longer, and it ended with a prayer offered by one of the recovering addicts. Then everyone walked out into the evening sunset.

July

The best-known hangout for the homeless, the mentally ill, and the drug-addicted in Salt Lake City was Pioneer Park. And though it was a well-known hub for drugs and homelessness, the city kept the park looking like it was made for families and small children. It was filled with large old trees, benches, a top-notch playground, lots of sidewalks.

Police patrolled the park constantly, and the city planned events such as farmers markets and concerts to attract less sketchy crowds. Despite efforts to rid the park of the homeless and the mentally ill, and of all the predators and parasites that preyed on them, the park was still a main gathering place for them. Its location near the central train terminal and Salt Lake City's largest homeless shelters probably didn't help the city's efforts to clear up the problems.

Matthew minded his own business and was left alone except for the occasional drug dealer. He sat on a bench in the shade and tapped a foot rapidly. He frequently rubbed the patch of red, swollen and bleeding skin on his forehead and jerked his head one way, then the other. Beside him on the bench sat his large backpack, stuffed to overflowing.

"I've got to go," Matthew said. "Got to go, now!"

A voice spoke back. "Where to?"

"Away!" Matthew shouted.

"I'm your companion," the voice said. "I stay with you no matter where you go or what you do. Where can you go?"

Just then, a shadowy hand fell on his shoulder, and a raspy whisper spoke in his ear. "That woman there. You see her?"

Matthew saw her. A slender, or gaunt, if truth be told, red head. She wore a blue tank-top, a black skirt, and flip-flops. Her white skin showed the veins in her legs and in the exposed parts of her chest and back. Her hair was pulled back and tied in a bun. Her smile had several black gaps. She did not seem to have any belongings.

"You could do things to her," the voice said. "And she would do things to you. All it would cost is a bit of your time."

"No. I've got to go." Matthew said.

"Oh, you don't have to do it if you don't want to do it. But you want to do it. It's exactly what you want to do."

Matthew rose from the bench.

"You could probably do everything right here in the park," said the voice. "Do you think she would like that?"

"No," Matthew said. He watched the woman interact with another man, apparently a boyfriend or a husband.

"Do you feel it? Do you feel that you want her?"

Another voice from behind Matthew, another shadow, said, "Yes, you do. You want her."

The red-headed woman gazed at Matthew. "You want this?" She rubbed her breasts seductively. Her face changed form to become a snake's face, dotted with scales, with yellow eyes with vertical black pupils. "Yessss," the snake's head said, "Come!"

Matthew saw shadows everywhere, they watched him from the trees, from the tops of buildings, from the cars that passed by. They moved in mobs toward him from all sides.

"Boy! You okay?" A demon, or a man, or something, stood before him. Its white, powdered face and red eyes, its bonfire hair, its naked and bloodied body. "You okay, boy?"

Matthew fled with his backpack and pulled the straps around his shoulders as he ran. He paid no attention to traffic signs but thought only of fleeing the shadows and voices.

$$\Omega$$

Crack the egg on the counter, like this." Kristi was in the kitchen with an egg in her hand. And Audrey, who only stood about a head taller than the countertop, watched, as Kristi cracked the egg with a single strike and pulled apart the two halves. The white and yolk fell in one mass into the steel mixing bowl. "See? Not too hard. Try it."

Audrey cracked an egg on the countertop and soon it fell into the bowl too.

"Good! What's next?" Kristi asked.

Audrey read the recipe. "We mix for three to four minutes."

Kristi turned on the mixer.

Just then Susan turned the corner into the kitchen. She held a rag and a bottle of wood polish. "It's so good to see you two in the kitchen together." She opened the cabinet beneath the sink and put the wood polish away.

"We're making chocolate cake!" Audrey said.

"Cake, huh?" Susan said. "Are you going to share that cake?"

"Yep," Audrey said. She was on her tiptoes and peered into the mixing bowl.

Susan smiled and walked out of the kitchen.

"Hey, Grandpa!" Audrey said.

David's voice, from somewhere in the house shouted back, "Yeah?"

"You want some chocolate cake too?"

"I sure do." He flushed a toilet. "Fixed it! Guest bathroom is up and running again."

"Thanks hon!" Susan said.

"Thanks dad!" Kristi said.

"Thanks grandpa!" Audrey said.

Kristi turned off the mixer, lifted the bowl out, and poured the batter into the cake pan. Audrey used a rubber spatula to scrape the sides.

"Okay Audrey, what's next?"

Audrey took a minute to read. "We bake it for thirty to thirty-five minutes."

"Is the oven ready?"

"Yep!"

"Okay, here goes." Kristi opened the oven, and slid the cake pan onto the rack.

August

For three days Matthew sat a dozen yards from the road just outside of Nephi, surrounded by his scattered belongings that were strewn around him. In the last several weeks he had abandoned his car and made it about eighty miles south of Salt Lake City before he was overcome by the things that haunted him. On State Highway 132, less than a mile from Interstate

Fifteen, the voices, visions and distortions kept him from moving far from where his things were spread. He had not taken food or water. Hunger and dehydration worsened the symptoms.

Commuters saw him. Sherriff's deputies and Highway Patrol officers passed by, but nobody stopped to help or ask questions.

"What's wrong with him?" some children asked from the back seats of several cars. Parents said, "He's homeless. He made some bad choices."

Some drivers winced, and some even thought to pull over and ask, "Is everything okay?" But nobody did.

During his third night on the roadside, his skin blistered by the sun, Matthew walked away from his place in the dirt among the sagebrush, away from all his belongings, and wandered along the road's white line.

Ω

Kristi was traveling home from Delta with Audrey in the back seat. The highway that wound around the curves of the shallow canyon was as familiar to her as family. She had traveled it hundreds of times in her life, and she knew every turn and every tree, and where to watch for deer.

The digital clock on the dash read ten thirty-two. She had plenty of time to get home before her eleven o'clock curfew.

Her phone buzzed. Its light glowed inside her purse on the passenger's seat. She retrieved it and glanced at the display.

In the brief seconds that she lost her focus on the road, the car wavered along the white line where a man happened to walk, and Kristi saw him too late to brake or swerve.

Inside the car the collision sounded like an explosion. She watched him, as if in slow motion, thrown into the right frame of her windshield before he disappeared over the top of the car.

She locked the brakes, and the steering wheel spun out of her hands. The car swerved precipitously to the left before Kristi overcorrected to the right, and the car spun around then came to a stop just off the road. The headlights shone on the sagebrush and the oaks in the direction from which she had just come. On the road lay the broken pieces of the car's side mirror.

Neither Kristi nor her daughter uttered a sound. Kristi's stomach became a knot, and she felt like vomiting. She turned to Audrey and tried to appear calm. "Are you okay?"

Audrey looked at her mother with wide, unblinking eyes, and nodded.

Kristi picked the phone up off the floor and saw the missed call from her mother.

The passenger's side of the windshield was cracked into a thousand crystals but remained intact, and the side-view mirror was missing. The frame had taken most of the impact.

Kristi watched the roadside and saw nothing but a calm summer night. She unbuckled her seatbelt and opened the door. "Stay here," she said.

She left the door open and ignored the digital alarm reminding her the key was in the ignition, and she walked in the light of the headlamps, scanning the feral wheat grass and the gravel at the roadside.

"Hello?" she said.

There was no answer.

She arrived at the site of the crash, where pieces of her side mirror lay. She picked up a piece of plastic that used to hold the glass, and she looked farther into the scrub oaks and the sagebrush where the headlights cast their yellow glow.

When she saw nothing out of the ordinary, an emotion, something like hope, or relief, began to rise inside her. She felt compelled to turn back to the car and drive away. She had hit a deer, that was all.

Then the sound of gurgling cut into the night. Suddenly, Kristi could not breathe, could not move. She dropped the piece of plastic, and it bounced on the asphalt. The world converged on her chest, all the sounds were hollow, and stood motionless until her panic was interrupted by approaching headlights.

A pickup rounded the curve, slowed and pulled over, and blinded Kristi with its high beams. A man opened the door, placed one foot on the ground, and shouted so that his voice was heard over his truck's loud engine, "Are you okay?"

"I...I hit a deer," Kristi yelled back.

The man looked around. "Must've run off."

"Yeah. I think so."

"Is your car running? Do you need any help?"

"Yes, it's running. I'm okay."

After a few steps backward, Kristi turned back to her car. She tried hard not to seem shaken, and her instincts told her to run fast and far away from the scene, but she forced herself to walk calmly.

The truck pulled away.

Kristi turned back after the truck was well on its way, and she walked down the gentle slope through the yellow feral wheat, and she approached the shrubs where she now knew the man lay. She could hear his labored breaths as blood filled his throat, and she followed the sound into the sagebrush.

She was now only a few steps away from him. His eyes glistened in the bits of light that made its way through the brush. Blood trickled from his mouth. One leg was folded unnaturally beneath him. His other leg was bent over a bush. His arms were spread straight out, palms up.

Kristi stepped a bit closer and instinctively thought to help, but she stopped herself. It was too late. The man was drowning in his own blood.

"I'm so sorry," Kristi said in a whisper. "I'm so very sorry. It will be over soon. The pain will be gone soon."

The man moaned.

When Kristi heard the moan she shuddered, hurried forward, and kneeled a few feet away. "I'm here," she said. "I have a daughter...up there, in the car. She needs me." She
held back a sob. "I hope you underst—"

She could not finish the sentence but could only watch as the blood bubbled from his mouth, as he drowned in it, as his life became fainter, as his blood drained out more slowly, and he finally became still.

"Mom?" Audrey had stepped out of the car. She was crying.

Kristi stood up so Audrey could see her face in the light. "It's okay sweetie. We...we hit a deer. Stay in the car. I'll be right there." She backed away from the body until it was hidden by the brush, then turned and ran to the car, stumbling over stones in the grass along the way.

Once back in the driver's seat, the door was shut, and Kristi dialed 9-1-1. But she did not press *Send*.

What had seemed right suddenly felt wrong. What might police do when they saw her criminal history? Certainly, she would be prosecuted, and as always, found guilty. Would she be charged with murder? Kristi mulled these and other thoughts. She was unable to comprehend any positive outcomes, and every possibility that came to mind seemed more terrible than the last one.

In her mirror, she could see her daughter crying. Audrey had not been fooled.

Kristi put her phone away, then took some deep breaths and tried to think through her options. "Let's say a prayer. Do you think a prayer can help?"

"Okay," Audrey said.

They bowed their heads, and closed their eyes and Kristi prayed to God, whom she had been taught would never give her a trial she could not overcome.

"Heavenly Father," Kristi began, "please help." There was a long pause. Kristi couldn't think of anything to say. "Father, we have been through so much, and we can't deal with this. It can't happen. We've come so far. If there are miracles, we pray for a miracle now. Help this go away. In the name of Jesus Christ. Amen."

The two sat in silence until Audrey spoke. "Mom, what are we going to do?"

"I don't know," Kristi said.

"Will we get in trouble?"

"Nothing will happen to you, sweetie."

"But how about you, mom?"

Kristi looked in the mirror and saw Audrey wiping her cheeks. "I think everything will be okay," she said.

"Who is he?" Audrey asked.

"He...he was just a homeless man. Probably on drugs."

"Is he a bad man?"

"I think he...I don't know."

"If he was a bad man, and we call the police, will you get in trouble, mom?"

"I don't know. Probably."

"Will you go to jail?"

"I think so."

"Even if he was a bad man?"

"Yes."

Kristi turned to face Audrey. "What we're going to do has nothing to do with you. Nothing will ever happen to you because of this. I promise. You're going to be just fine. Okay?"

"Okay, mom."

Kristi buckled her seatbelt. Then she turned the key, shifted the car into gear, and drove away.

Signs And Wonders

On a hot August morning, a young husband and wife, still in their early twenties, climbed up a steep mountain slope through the narrow floor of a ravine. Despite their youth their brows were set low in pensive scowls. Carl wore an expressionless frown. Madeline wore a half-smile that contrasted with her eyes. They were married for nearly two years.

Like all ravines in the Wasatch Mountain range, this one was cut by thousands of spring snow melts and rainfalls. In all those years the sporadic streams flowed through it, and eventually emptied into the rivers of Utah Valley, went on to Utah Lake, funneled into the Jordan River, then died in the Great Salt Lake and floated to the sky.

In mid-August on that hot blue-sky day there was no sign of water. The rounded stones, the broken granite boulders, the sand, the yellow grass, all soaked up heat and gave any moisture back to the atmosphere.

Carl and Madeline pushed through the stands of scrub oak whose crooked branches scratched at their legs and chests. They climbed over or around the granite boulders that had tumbled down the ravine's sloped walls. They climbed over piles of shifting rocks or shifting sand or held onto sturdy branches to pull themselves over crags and cliffs. Their hands, shins, t-shirts, shorts, and shoes were covered with dust and scratches.

Carl led the way, occasionally walking through spider webs that stretched from scraggly oak to scraggly oak. The sticky silk filaments stuck to him and he gasped in surprise, dropped the shovel he was carrying, and flailed his hands until he was convinced the spiders were gone.

Although Madeline stayed several yards behind her husband, she hiked the terrain expertly. Her breathing was heavy, but the work was not much harder than an early morning run. She watched Carl from behind, how his shoulders sagged, how he hunched and gasped for breath, and how his blue t-shirt was soaked with sweat as he stumbled awkwardly along.

Madeline frequently stepped aside to allow little stone avalanches to roll past, because Carl did not seem to know how to find a sure footing. And whenever he slipped and rolled the stones, he looked back to make sure she was okay. "I'm sorry," he always said with pained eyes. "It's okay," Madeline would say.

Carl leaned on the shovel from time to time as if he might soon fall over. When he took breaks from the climb he dropped the shovel, held his hands behind his head, and interrupted his heavy breathing with high pitched groans, low pitched groans, and half-expressed complaints about the trek, and how from the valley below the path appeared deceptively smooth and easy, and how maybe the ridge above them would have been easier to climb.

During these breaks Madeline stopped too, always several yards behind Carl. She wiped her forehead with her shirt sleeve then looked to the valley below and made small talk. Even after two hours of climbing she felt as ready to chat as she had before they began the climb.

"The houses look so small, don't they Carl?" said Madeline during one of the short breaks.

"Uh-huh." Carl said. He squinted from the sting of hair gel carried into his eyes by his sweat. "It's not too far now." He picked up the shovel and continued climbing.

"Carl, I hoped you'd have given up on this by now. Do you really think you're going to find—"

"I saw it Maddie," Carl said. "I don't think anything. I know...I know with every fiber of my being. It's right up here. I think I can see it with my spiritual eyes."

Madeline had once believed in visions and angels, and had honored the authority of Carl's priesthood, vested on him by the church. Yet, when Carl really began to study and pray, and began having visions and seeing angels, and reaping the divine blessings of the priesthood, she turned the other way and doubted. Carl was unsure how to reason with her now.

"Well," Madeline said, "there are lots of places that look like this. Your dream could have been anything, really. Seeing granite on a mountain in a dream. Well, these mountains are granite. There's granite everywhere. Of course you would dream about granite mountains—"

"I said I know it's here. That means I know. Also, it wasn't a dream, okay? It was a vision." He rubbed his eyes with dirty fingers. "Why did you even come up here with me if you're just going to doubt? Have some faith in me." She could at least let him be and stop interfering!

"Faith? Carl, I came to make sure you don't get yourself killed. That's the only reason. If you want me to talk about my faith, here it is. I have no faith in any of this. Not the tiniest shred of faith. In fact, I think you've turned crazy over this old story. Nobody in my family has ever taken it seriously."

"Maddie, you've got to have faith. That's how God works. What we're doing is his will for us. It's just like Abraham when the Lord promised him the land of Canaan. He didn't actually inherit Canaan, remember? In fact, he died without receiving God's promise. It took hundreds of years, literally hundreds, before Israel inherited the place."

"Carl, what the heck are you talking about?" Madeline said.

Carl hung his head and sighed. He and Madeline used to talk late into the night about the blessings of the gospel, about the deeper doctrine of the scriptures. Yet now she couldn't understand. "You see," Carl said, "your ancestor was like Abraham and we are the heirs of the promise, the promise God made to your great-great-great-great grandfather. Spanish gold! Nephite gold! So, when he received his revelation about the gold in these mountains, he never got it. That wasn't God's will. But now here we are, his heirs, just like Israel was heirs to Abraham. Our inheritance is in this mountain. I'm certain it's right up there, just a little higher."

He squinted into the sky, then wiped his face and rubbed his sweat-stung eyes again with his hand. "Let me put it this way, I'm like Joshua, and you're Israel. I'm the one with unshakeable faith, and you're—don't take this the wrong way Maddie—but you waver a lot. Sometimes you're faithful, and sometimes you're building idols to false gods. I just don't understand you anymore. You've lost the faith you had when we got married. But soon, very soon, you will see God's promise, like when Thomas saw Jesus. And then, like Thomas, you'll believe again." He stepped onto a boulder that blocked his way "Maddie, God desires happiness for you. And that happiness is waiting just up there. A new life. I promise. Come on."

Madeline fired back. "Carl, you've lost your faith too. The simple kind of faith you had when we got married. You're not the man I married. You're going to get hurt or killed wandering around in the mountains like this. And you're not going to find anything. You've been out here every night and every weekend for months, Carl. Months! Well, there's nothing here but weeds and rocks. God didn't give you a revelation, and I don't believe he gave my ancestor a revelation. I think you gave yourselves revelations!"

Carl said, "But...but, I'm like the prophet Lehi and you're like his wife, Sariah. When Sariah lost faith and thought their sons were dead—"

"Carl! Shut up!" Madeline said.

Carl turned, sulking, and continued up through the rocks and brush. Madeline let out a frustrated groan and followed. They weaved through a grove of scrub oak, and over a field of broken rock, and faced a small outcrop of granite. Carl climbed up first, then Madeline, and they found themselves on a small parcel of flat ground covered with riverbed stones, sand, gravel, and wild raspberry bushes.

While Madeline admired the raspberries and commented on what she described as a "little oasis," Carl stepped forward and stared with wonder at a chunk of granite that jutted out of the mountain. It was an ominous presence that seemed as if it might reveal a mouth and begin to utter warnings.

"This is it! This is the right place." Carl let go of the shovel, and it teetered on the spade's edge, tipped over, and clattered on the rocks. He moved into the shadow of the granite boulder and placed his hands on the cool surface. It stood twice Carl's height, and it was as wide as it was tall. "See how flat this side is, Maddie? Definitely carved by man!" He touched his forehead to it, closed his eyes, and whispered a hasty prayer of gratitude. Then he began sliding his hands up, down and across, looking for signs in every bump and crack.

Madeline returned to the edge of the clearing where grass had grown and yellowed on a small bank of sand, and she looked down at the ravine they had climbed. Then she looked higher up the mountain, to see a forest of dead gray pines. "Oh, my gosh," she whispered. "It's like the end of the world."

"What?"

"Nothing. Just thinking out loud."

"Hey, Maddie, look at this." Carl had explored the side of the boulder, near where it jutted out from the mountain. He pointed at a vertical crack that split the flat side from the rest of the outcrop. "See this? This thing isn't a big rock. It only *looks* like a big rock. It's man-made! See here? If we just tip this front part over, the cave is just behind it."

Madeline came closer, looked at the granite, glanced at her husband, then again at the granite. "I don't think it's anything but a rock. It's just a broken rock, Carl."

"No, look," Carl said. "It's almost a perfect line. The Nephites only made imperfections on purpose to keep anyone from finding it. This is definitely man-made." Carl ran his fingers along the crack, "Definitely man-made."

"How do you know it's man-made? Look, here it just looks like an old, jagged crack."

"Do you think I'm stupid, Maddie?"

Madeline turned back to the patch of grass and looked out over the valley. She watched the cars and trucks as they moved north and south along the interstate, and on the Main Streets and State Highways. Cars flowed in long endless columns in every direction.

Carl took the shovel in hand with renewed confidence, then stretched out his arms like an Old Testament prophet in a painting, who preaches to a multitude of wayward souls. "Maddie, your ancestor saw the promise, but he wasn't righteous enough to get it. And so, your family wandered in the wilderness all these years. But you and me, Maddie, we're the righteous ones, so we inherit the promise."

"I don't think my ancestors were unrighteous," Madeline said. "They were good people, all of them."

"Well, how else do you explain any of this?" Carl said. "You've got to think about that, Maddie. How do you explain us finding this? It's our righteousness that brought us here. We are worthy of it."

"Look up there," said Madeline, pointing at the stone outcrops above. "There's probably a hundred just like it. See?"

"No, not like this one. Look at it. There's not a sharp edge on the whole rock."

"Yes, there is, Carl. Lots of them. Look there." Madeline pointed.

"Well, okay. It's not perfect. But only because the stone carvers were smart enough to disguise it."

Madeline did not respond for more than a minute, and when she did, her voice was soft and thoughtful, and her words seemed far from the topic. "Isn't the valley pretty, Carl? There are so many good people down there. Beautiful people."

Carl looked over the valley. He felt overwhelmed by the thoughts of the drug addictions, the pornography, and the other vices he knew existed in Utah Valley. "Beautiful?" He shook his head, trying to shake off the nonsense. "Maddie, right now I feel like Jesus when he was on the mountain overlooking Jerusalem, and he said, 'Jerusalem, Jerusalem, how long have I tried to gather you like a hen gathers her chicks.' I feel just like Jesus must have felt. That's what I see when I look down there."

Madeline ignored him. Instead, she continued to watch the towns and cities, the roads, Utah Lake. Mt. Nebo in the distance had a white strip of winter snow still lingering just below one of the north-facing slopes.

"Well, you go ahead and think whatever you want," Carl said. "I'm going to have faith." He turned back to the rock and slapped it. "It's just behind this. See? See here? And here? See? It's obvious if you would just look, Maddie."

"I see a big broken rock," Madeline said.

Carl squatted for a closer look, exploring the wide crack with a forefinger. "All I've got to do is make this front piece fall."

He kneeled beside the rock and wedged the shovel into the crack, then pushed the shovel's handle hoping to tip the rock, but nothing moved. Next, he climbed the steep hillside and stepped on top of the rock. "Better leverage up here," he said, in case Madeline was listening.

Madeline remained seated on the grass. She leaned back on her hands and looked down at the white "U" on her red University of Utah shirt. Then, after she brushed some dust off her shoes, she turned her face skyward, into the sun.

Carl took a break, climbed back down, and sat beside her. "You know, when we get the gold, you can go back to college. To BYU."

Madeline threw a glance. Of all schools, BYU was the antithesis of the University of Utah. "Sure," she said. "BYU."

"What's the matter?" Carl asked.

"Nothing."

"That's what we'll do then. First thing we'll do is get you back into college. And I'll pay for it."

Carl went back to his place on the rock, where the shovel stood wedged into the crack. He pulled on the handle until the wood began to pop, then he pushed outward, but the rock did not budge. He pushed the shovel farther into the crack, and tried pushing again, pressing his chest against the handle, applying all his weight.

With a single loud pop, the shovel's handle broke, and Carl fell face first onto the gravel below. A puff of dust blew out from beneath him when he hit the ground. He rolled over and gasped for air.

Madeline rushed to his side. "Are you okay? Are you hurt?"

Carl held out his hand, unable to speak for the moment. He rolled over and soon caught his breath. "I'm okay."

The shovel's handle had broken diagonally at a shallow angle so that it was pointed at one end and looked something like a wooden sword.

"This might work better anyway," Carl said. "I'm going to get some dirt out of the crack first, I think."

Madeline returned to the yellow grass and watched Carl limp back up the hill and onto the rock. He began to poke around inside the crack with the shovel's broken handle. The sun was in the center of the sky by then and even the raspberry bushes that lined the wall across from where Carl worked were not shaded at midday.

Carl worked at his task of scraping dirt and debris, then he pushed the sharp end of the handle deep into the crack and pushed with his heels. He kicked, and pushed, and kicked some more until he was out of breath.

Suddenly he saw the slightest bit of movement. "Did you see that? Did you see it move?"

"I saw it!" Madeline was more surprised than Carl. Before she saw the tiny shift of the rock, she had been faithless. But now...what if...

Carl jumped onto the hillside and was soon at Madeline's side. "This is it, Maddie. This is it!"

"Well, maybe it is."

"Yes! Maddie, just have faith."

He knelt in front of the rock where he imagined the entrance to the cave would be. It seemed to stare down on him like an angry god as he looked up at the sky, clasped his hands and closed his eyes. "Heavenly Father, we thank thee for bringing us here. We thank thee that—"

"Carl!" Madeline cried. She had not kneeled with him, but stood to the side, watching. And she watched the broken slab tip over like a tree.

Carl looked up, just in time to see the danger. He fell backward and held up his hands for protection. But in a moment, with the sound of a thunderclap and a cloud of dust, the slab of rock lay flat on the ground.

Madeline leaped up and found herself frantically lifting and pushing. She cried for Carl to respond, as if by a miracle he was alive beneath it and would come out unscathed and glad to still be among the living.

She began to scoop away at the gravel and the riverbed stones closest to where she had last seen him. Soon her hands and fingertips were cut and bleeding, but she continued until she saw Carl's blood seep out from beneath his granite tomb. Then she sat back and watched it expand in the gravel.

When the blood stopped creeping out from under the rock, Madeline kneeled and wept. She repeated Carl's name again and again and apologized for anything she believed that she had done to hurt him. Her sobs echoed against the mountainside and dissipated into the air.

In a moment of curiosity, she looked at the broken rock. There was no door to riches behind the broken slab of granite. Just more solid granite.

Finally, she let herself fall backward, and she lay on her back staring at the sky until her sobs subsided. Then she crawled to the edge of the little oasis, retrieved the phone from her pocket, and dialed 9-1-1.

After she answered numerous questions and described her location, she sat on the grass and tilted her phone back and forth, reflecting the sun's light into the valley.

In the valley below rescuers looked eastward until they saw the light.

Hearts of The Children

An old man in his eighties, and a woman at least twenty years younger, sat across from each other in the old man's living room on matching blue chairs with floral print. A wide coffee table sat between them. On the table, glasses of water sat on coasters, and a plate of cookies lay untouched.

The woman, Teresa Cardon, glanced around while they made introductory small talk. "Your home is very well preserved, Mr. Heath," she said.

"We've spent a lot of time and money on this place," Martin said. "When we bought it, it was pretty run down. But we've preserved as much as possible." He tapped his foot on the floor, "This isn't the original wood," he said, "but we got it from another old house and installed it here. So, the floor is about as old as the house."

"How old?" Teresa asked.

"About a hundred and twenty years." Martin said. "We pulled off all the old plaster on the interior walls, put in some new framing and wiring, and sheet rock. But if you noticed, we've put plaster over the sheet rock so it looks older." He pointed at the trim, the doorframes, and the window frames. "That's all original. We pulled it all out, and we did the remodeling, and we put it all back in, with only a few adjustments."

"Sounds like a lot of work," Teresa said. She checked the time on her phone.

"It was. But you know, here in Utah people just knock these old places down and build their big lifeless mansions. Those of us who are able to preserve these places, to preserve our heritage, should do it."

Teresa nodded her head in agreement.

Martin scratched his left forearm then straightened the sleeve of his sweater. "Where did you say you're from?"

"I live in Layton."

Teresa was observing a large painting that hung on the wall, depicting Jesus in a post-apocalyptic Washington D.C. In the painting Jesus held the United States Constitution in his hand, raising it up for all to see. Far in the background were prominent buildings from the United States capitol, and directly behind Jesus was a multitude of soldiers and famous politicians from United States History. In the foreground, to Jesus's right, gazing at Jesus and praising him, were a mother with a child, a farmer, a man who held a book titled *The Five Thousand Year Leap*, and a United States Marine who held a folded flag.

To Jesus's left was another group, bearing darker shadows and looking away from him. A man held a copy of *Origin of Species* by Charles Darwin, a robed judge had his face in his hands and court documents were scattered around him, a pregnant woman's left hand clearly showed the absence of a ring, a young man counted a pile of money, and a shadowy demonic figure stood in their midst. On the dark wood frame, a bronze plaque was engraved with the words *One Nation Under God*.

"You like McNaughton?" Martin asked.

"Who?"

"The artist who painted that." Martin gestured to the painting.

"Well…I've never seen his work before," Teresa said.

"He's a faithful member of the church. And I believe he's inspired by the Holy Ghost."

Teresa changed the subject. "Do you mind if we take a look at some of the letters?"

"Oh, of course." Martin went into the office adjacent to the living room and continued to talk while he retrieved the scrapbook. "You know, I never knew I had a cousin in Layton. We have a reunion every five years, and I thought I knew all my relatives. But I've never seen you. Our family trees must've diverged pretty soon after arriving in Utah."

"I think you're right," said Teresa. "I think my ancestor was the black sheep of the family. I'm just now discovering all you guys."

"We're a pretty close family," said Martin. He was still in the office, flipping through the scrapbook's pages, taking a quick look before he handed them over. "You could be close to us too. You could come to the reunion next year. More than two hundred people show up, and it grows every year because babies are born, you know, and kids get married. You should come."

"I'd like that," Teresa said. "My family reunions are pretty sparse. My brother and my aunts, and their families. That's about it."

Martin walked back into the living room and passed Teresa the book.

Teresa hefted it. It was so filled with letters, photographs and legal documents, that the pages splayed out wider than the two-inch binding. She laid it on her lap and turned to the first document, then to the second, third and fourth.

The first letters were correspondences to or from Enoch Heath, Martin and Teresa's common ancestor.

Enoch's Mormon conversion story was a well-known part of family lore. He had been a charismatic protestant pastor in England before he was converted by two missionaries who happened upon his church one Sunday. According to the story, he received a divine revelation in 1900 in which he was commanded by God to join Mormonism and flee to Utah in preparation for the second coming of Jesus Christ. The family sold all their holdings, took their cash fortune, and by boat and train arrived in Utah. The story of Enoch Heath's inspiring conversion had been passed down to his descendants, with a few variations in supernatural details.

Teresa adjusted her glasses and flipped through the book a few pages at a time, glancing at dates and places, 1884, 1890, 1901, 1943, and 1964, and Edinburgh, London, New York, Salt Lake City, and Malad, Idaho. Documents were glued, taped or loosely inserted between the pages, and every so often she lifted one out to glance at it.

When she had flipped through the whole folder, she turned back to the beginning. "This...this is wonderful," she said.

"Yes, yes, it is quite a collection," he said. "My mother found people from as far away as England, who helped her compile it."

Teresa prepared to take notes, and she began to read the first page again. But Martin interrupted.

"Do you have any grandchildren?"

Teresa glanced over the rim of her glasses. She had not really introduced herself to Martin, and did not want to be rude. She closed the book.

"No grandkids. Not yet," she said. "And you?"

"Seventeen. And a great-grandson," he said. "No grandchildren?"

"My oldest is twenty-seven," Teresa said, "She's working on her PhD at the U. She's not married yet. My son is twenty-five, and he got married last summer. They're waiting to have kids until he's done with school. So, no grandkids for a while yet."

"And only two children?"

"Yes."

"Well, everyone has their own preferences."

"I suppose we do," Teresa said. "Everyone's different."

"I was blessed with six children," Martin said. "My sons served missions in Russia, India, El Salvador and Portland. My youngest, who went to Portland..." Martin spent several minutes talking about the Portland mission, as if trying to justify why his son was sent there instead of someplace else. He explained that serving in Portland gave his son skills that perfectly suited his now lucrative career. And he said, "the Lord will call his missionaries to wherever he needs them, whether it's Russia or Portland." He summarized the success of his children, saying, "All my kids are married in the Logan temple. That's where me and my wife were married, too."

Teresa said, "A family tradition. How nice."

"We've all been true to our temple covenants," Martin said.

"I'm glad your kids haven't given you much trouble."

"They're all pretty good kids. Three of my sons have been bishops, and one of them is in the Stake Presidency. I've had seven grandchildren serve missions so far."

"Looks like you did a good job," Teresa said.

"I think so. When parents are righteous and raise their children in the church, their children and grandchildren will not depart from it."

Teresa cleared her throat and said, "Sounds like you have an amazing family." If ever a wayward child fell from Martin

Heath's family tree, he certainly never mentioned it to Teresa. She tried to ignore the thought that Martin was trying to establish his spiritual superiority.

Some moments of silence passed. Teresa was no fan of small talk or of boasting. And she shifted uncomfortably in the silence.

Martin sat up straight in the recliner. "On the phone, you mentioned you were looking for names to submit to the temple."

"Uh-huh, yes," Teresa said.

"Before you continue, I want you to know that you won't find anyone in that book that needs temple work. All the temple work has been finished. My mother was meticulous about it." Martin settled into his soft chair and folded his fingers on his flat belly.

"I understand what you're saying," Teresa said. "Sometimes when you think you've seen everything from every angle, just when you think you're finished, suddenly another name pops up, or a date, or a place. You can find yourself taking a tiny clue and discovering another ancestor whose temple work hasn't been done."

Martin lowered his brows. "Just know," he said, "no matter what you find, all the work that should be done has been done."

"That's alright. Even if I don't find any new names for the temple, I still like to learn about people. I've become obsessed with family history. Not just temple work for the dead, but with history itself. I love the wheres, whens and hows of history, especially when it's family. But what most fascinates me are the whys. Why did so-and-so do this or that? What were his motives? That's what really gets me excited."

Martin said nothing. The stranger in his home was about to get a lesson in family history.

Teresa opened the book again and started to read.

Martin thumbed through some mail that sat on a side table, which was addressed to Dr. Martin Heath. He began ripping open the tops of envelopes and noisily unfolding the letters and bills. He glanced up every few seconds to watch Teresa. When he finished reading a piece of mail, he crumpled it and laid it back on the table, and soon had a small pile of crumpled pages.

Meanwhile, Teresa read a letter from 1860, then turned the page and read the next and the next. She took notes as she went and wrote dozens of little details in her notebook. "1864, Enoch Heath, Edinburgh to Jane, London. Edinburgh is 'a windswept wasteland.'" "1864, Jane Heath, London to Enoch. 'My son. God is with you. Be not afraid.'" "Enoch Heath, London, to James MacCarran, New York, 1880, seeking to invest in railroad stock." "Enoch Heath, Sermon, 1884, 'God speaks to every soul,' 'Satan appears almost as an angel of light,' 'Obedience.'" "Enoch Heath to Nestor Heath, 1888, 'Warm regards from Margaret and me, and from our five children.'"

Forty minutes had passed and no words were spoken between the two distant cousins. No water had been drunk, no cookies eaten. Only the shuffling and crumpling of paper and the turning of pages. Martin finished reading his mail and sat watching Teresa.

Teresa tapped the point of her pen on the notepad. She had stopped reading. "Mr. Heath—"

"Please, call me Martin. We're family, aren't we?"

"Okay. Martin," she said. "Enoch mentions here to his brother that he has five children. I only know of four."

"Yes, yes. Originally, five. The child you never heard of is Enoch's son Robert."

Teresa shook her head. "I've never heard of him. I've seen all the temple ordinance records, and I've never seen a 'Robert' among them."

"There are good reasons you haven't seen his name in your research," said Martin. "After the Heaths came to Utah, they never mentioned him. And he…" Martin drifted off into his thoughts. "I think you'll find Robert's letter in the next few pages. It'll all be pretty clear once you know."

Martin picked up a leather-bound copy of *A Tale of Two Cities* that decorated his coffee table, and thumbed through it, pretending to read.

Teresa skipped ahead a few pages and found Robert Heath's letter. She looked the letter over and placed her finger on the address scribbled at the top of the first page, "Is this it? This one from Dartmoor *Prison*?"

"That's the one."

8 November, 1899
Dartmoor Prison, Princetown, Dover

Dear father and mother,

> *Months have passed and I have hesitated to write for fear you have not understood my calling. But today is my last day on this earth, and I can wait no longer. I shall endeavor to recount the history of my calling and why I carried it out, so you might have*

great hope of our reunion at the great white throne of God in His Kingdom.

The day I fulfilled my calling was as beautiful as imaginable—one of the rare, sun-filled days of the season. Beams from the sky blended with the slight chill in the air for a perfect warmth on the skin. People walked about campus for the sheer joy of it.

I arrived at my office soon after sunrise and looked down at the students and my fellow lecturers from my window on the third floor. They flowed like rivers and streams to their respective classes.

Aware that I might teach without incident I had prepared to lecture on Satan's democratic governance as portrayed in Milton's Paradise Lost, *contrasted with the tyranny of God's governance—as Satan saw it, of course—in the Kingdom of God. The lecture was worthy to stand alongside the finest literary analyses and criticisms of all time, even if I am only twenty-four years old.*

Dear mother and father, imagine the gravity and enlightenment of my lectures had I lived to forty! As always you would have praised the lecture, for you have eternally been my greatest supporters.

My notes were well organized and I was intent on delivering them to my students that day. I was also prepared to fulfill my calling at any moment. One never knows when God will say, "My son, do your duty!" and so I had everything arranged for that eventuality.

During the trial, you were made aware of my actions on that day. You were apprised of the weaponry I had concealed in various places for the occasion. You heard, perhaps, through your tears, how the lawyers all agreed— "the man is mad"—disagreeing only on the matter of my sentence—whether they should send me to an asylum or to my death.

Please be comforted, for I shall explain to you that I am not lost to insanity, but to the Kingdom of God.

Thirty sunrises prior to the foreordained day I had eased an astounding headache with a large dose of diamorphine and a glass of Scotch whiskey. While I sat before the fire and stared into the flames, waiting for the headache to subside, I thought I heard a voice calling my name from the fireplace by way of the chimney. At first, I believed that some prankster, likely a student, had climbed the wall and was pestering me from the rooftop, and I shouted profanities into the fireplace.

The voice carried on, however, beckoning me nearer. I perceived then the voice was far too calm and deep to be that of a prankster. When I came nearer the fireplace, I was dumbfounded to perceive it was the fire itself which spoke. In the moment, I recalled the story of God speaking to Moses from the fiery bush, and I remembered the numerous times father used that story in his sermons.

The fire unobtrusively repeated my name. My soul, it seemed, began to expand. All the religious teachings from my formative years passed in rapid succession through my mind. Father's sermons, which I am sad to say annoyed me to no end as a youth, of a sudden settled into the deepest recesses of my being, illuminating me from my center with a new and profound spiritual heart. In all my years of theological study, I never felt a deeper conviction than I did at that moment.

On my knees before the fire I clasped my hands together and wept, as the light of God filled me and overcame my human nature, replacing it with God's will. "I am here, Father!" I cried.

Then God spoke to me.

"I have a calling for thee, my son," said God. "Listen to my messenger."

A vision appeared in the fire: A rider mounted upon a pale horse burst forth in an explosion of sparks and smoke. He wore a robe dyed in blood. The features of his countenance were shadowed by a large hood that fell loosely to his brow. His face was gaunt, and the bones protruded from the starved, dried skin. Nonetheless he exuded the power of God; decayed lips firmly set, eyes black and piercing, physiognomy determined. He rode without saddle, stirrups or bridle, yet remained mounted despite the horse's rearing back and jerking about impatiently. In the angel's right hand, a double-bladed axe reflected the fire's light.

This was God's messenger of death, which you know from St. John's Apocalypse. His words were like thunder. And he informed me of my divine purpose. I was to be a messenger preceding Christ's coming.

I received one week of nightly visits from the angel of death, each preceded by a fervent headache. The angel *lectured from his horse as eloquently as Epicurus, employing every method of effective teaching. He showed me again and again, with great patience, until my calling was clear in my mind.*

One night no headache afflicted me, and I sat waiting for my teacher. All night I waited, until at about three o'clock in the morning. As I stoked the coals, I heard a faint voice; a whisper from the fire, that announced, "The field is white, ready to harvest."

For two weeks afterwards I prepared according to what my Lecturer taught me. The weaponry, as you saw evidenced in the trial, was diverse, never repeated; each knife a different size and shape; the swords different in length and width and hilt; the pistols all of a different make. Twelve weapons; that symbolic and significant number! At the end of two weeks I had concealed these tools throughout the campus, and I had planned my route carefully.

On the predestined morning, God called me to act by providing me a headache that I thought would end my life. As usual, I settled the pain with diamorphine and Scotch, as this mixture seems best for me. Then the voice of death's angel came like the ominous thunderclaps of our worst storms, "Today is the day of my wrath! Go! Be a fisher of men!" I placed my lecture notes in a drawer, for the lecture was not to be given.

I shall not recount the gruesome details you heard at the trial, for I know how you wept and how your hearts were terrorized with the descriptions and drawings and re-enactments. I only assure you that I did as you taught me from my earliest memories; I obeyed God.

Leaving my office I took the stairs as quickly as possible. The first weapon, a sword like those wielded by the fabled Samurai of Japan awaited me just beneath the soil outside the doors, and from thence I simply followed my plan.

The details of every disembowelment, the slitting of the throats from ear to ear, the bullets to the jugulars, I obeyed and performed. And at the twelfth; the ball of an antique pistol tearing through the throat of the last sacrifice, I was subdued by a mob.

My mission was complete. I was dragged violently away by police. I was beaten and thrown to the ground and shackled. But in the midst, you will be comforted to know I heard the voice of God say to me, "Well done, good and faithful servant!"

Tomorrow, soldiers of that latter-day Caesar who rules the New Babylon shall hang me by the neck. Not a soul has appealed on my behalf. Mine is a martyr's death. So be cheerful for me and not despairing, for I go to stand at the right hand of Christ, and shall be with Him at His coming.

I hope this letter gives you consolation, knowing that whatever befalls me, we shall meet again at the throne of God. Like you, I have been His obedient servant.

With love,
Your son, Robert

Teresa finished the letter, and whispered, "That's just—"

"Oh, he's not exactly a badge of pride for us," Martin said.

"But he doesn't show up in our genealogy. Why hasn't his temple work been done?"

"His work won't be done."

"Why not," Teresa said.

"He isn't worthy and can't ever be." Martin's jaw stiffened.

"You can't be serious."

"I am. We all are."

"Who is?"

"The family. All of us. His work will never be done."

Teresa glanced at the letter, and then back at Martin. "It is not our duty to judge who is worthy of saving ordinances," she said. "It's our duty to do the work for everyone, then let Christ figure out everything else. Nobody's left out. We need to have faith that everything will work out. And—"

"I had hoped it would be obvious after you read that letter," Martin said.

"That what would be obvious?"

"That you should not submit his name to the temple." Martin pointed to the book. "Go to the next page. There's a note from Enoch Heath about it. That'll help you understand."

Teresa turned the page and found a scrap of paper written in a nearly indecipherable cursive. It was dated September 1, 1902. She slowly read it and reviewed some scribbles three or four times, inserting possible interpretations for the scrawls, until it began to make sense.

On this day, 1 September Nineteen-Hundred-And-Two, I, Enoch Heath, by the authority of the priesthood, declare before gods, angels and these witnesses, in the Celestial room of the holy temple in Salt Lake City, Utah, that the name of Robert Heath, deceased on November 9, 1899 at Dartmoor Prison, England, shall never receive baptism or any other saving ordinance for as long as the fruit of my loins shall dwell upon the earth. I seal this blessing in the name of Jesus Christ. Amen.

The statement was signed by Enoch Heath, John Young, and George C. Maxwell.

"I...I've never heard of anything like this," Teresa said. "You don't think we should honor this, do you? The church would never recognize this."

"It was sealed with a priesthood blessing," Martin said. "An ordinance was performed in the temple, before witnesses."

"That wasn't an ordinance. You can't bestow a curse with a blessing," Teresa said.

"It's a seal that cannot be broken," Martin said.

"But Martin, it's not for us to decide who gets their temple work done. This note is ludicrous. The whole thing is—"

"Sister Cardon!"

"Yes, Martin?"

"As a faithful church member, don't you believe in the priesthood's power?"

"Yes, but—"

"And so, you believe it's the power to bind on earth and in heaven, and for all eternity?"

"Of course, but—"

"Then, don't defy the power of God! You would send a murderer to heaven. My brothers won't stand for it. My father and grandfather would not have stood for it either."

Teresa saw that Martin could not be reasoned with and closed the book. She had written the information she needed for her own research on Robert Heath.

She tried to end the visit on a lighter note. "Mr. Heath, I can see something has gone wrong today, and I'm sorry for any inconvenience I've caused you. You seem like a very nice man, and I know we disagree on a few things—"

"I need you to agree not to submit his name to the temple." Martin leaned forward and jabbed a pointed finger on the coffee table.

"No. I won't agree. It's ridiculous. And it's not Christ-like." She got up and walked toward the door.

Martin blocked Teresa's path. "You know what's not Christ-like? Dishonoring the priesthood isn't Christ-like. The Holy Ghost testifies the truth of this—"

"I do honor the priesthood, Mr. Heath! But I don't honor you, because you're not worthy of it. And I won't honor that ridiculous note or the devil who wrote it!" She walked around him and toward the door.

"Listen!" Martin said. He wrapped his thin hand around her arm.

Teresa jerked away, spun around to face him.

"I forbid you to get his temple work done," Martin said.

"You can't forbid that, and I think you know it."

"But what about the family? They'll see his baptism, his endowments, and—"

"The family? Is that the most important thing here? What about the worth of a soul?"

Martin stretched out his hands, pleading. "Family is the most important, Teresa. It's all we have, and it's all we can keep after this life. What you think is ridiculous is important to me and my relatives. If you could hold off for a few years, wait until some of us older folks die off. We're just not ready for it yet. Could you wait?"

"You want me to wait until you're dead?"

"Yes," said Martin, "If you will. When I'm gone, my older cousins and my brothers will be gone too. You see, if they see Robert's name on church records, they'll know it was me. I'm the only one who keeps Robert's records."

"And you're afraid they'll be angry with you if his temple work is done?"

"Yes, it would show up in the records and they'd see it. Sometimes for the sake of family you have to put off important work, leave it to future generations. Our grandchildren have never heard of Robert, and they won't care."

"Or," Teresa said, "You've got to do what is right, and let the consequence follow. Don't you believe that?"

Martin seemed much older now than he had just moments ago. Teresa observed that the bones on his face jutted out beneath his skin, his shoulders drooped, and his eyes stayed open only with great effort.

"I don't understand why your family would feel so strongly about this," Teresa said. "It makes no sense."

"I know it doesn't make sense to you," said Martin. "But it makes sense to those who honor the hopes and wishes of our ancestors."

"But wouldn't you agree we should do the work regardless of what other people think or feel about it?"

"It's more complicated than that," said Martin. "It's about the priesthood. It's about eternity and the family, and the will of God, and murder..." He seemed about to collapse and leaned on the back of a chair. "I can't stop you. You had better leave now."

Martin turned away, walked into the study, and closed the door behind him.

Teresa opened her notebook and read the information she wrote about Robert Heath. When she closed her notebook again, she said, "Thank you Mr. Heath, for your time today." Then she stepped outside and closed the door behind her and clicked the latch as when a parent closes the bedroom door of a sleeping child.

During Teresa's quiet drive home, the sun was far in the west and orange light filtered through the clouds and shone on the mountains, where tiny bright patches of red, orange and yellow had emerged among the deep green oaks, the maples, and the quaking aspen groves. Forests of dead pines, countless gray sticks, reached skyward, and forests of living pines showed the signs of fatigue and death. The traffic on Interstate Fifteen was thick but moved easily along at full speed. The sunset's light, as if through a stained-glass window, fell on the living, the dying, and the dead, and made them holy.

Sanctification

A boy, twelve years old, stepped down into the warm water and took his place beside an older man in the circular baptismal font. The man, the boy, and all the boys who sat on the bench awaiting their turns, wore identical white jumpsuits in various sizes.

The baptistery was well lit, and the marble floor was polished so that the light reflected from its flawless surface. With each baptism, the splash of immersion into the water and the cascade created when rising out of the water again echoed from the walls and ceiling and blended into a single sound. And though the baptist recited the baptismal prayer clearly, the echo in the room jumbled the words and made them unintelligible to everyone except the few who stood at the font. The whispers of boys who sat on the bench also rose into the air and spread across the room.

The font looked like a giant, ornate, white cauldron. It was set in a wide pit so that its rim was at floor level. The children stepped up to take their turns one by one, and they peered down into the well-lit hole to see that the font rested on the backs of twelve golden oxen.

For the twelve-year-old boy this was his first time in the temple. The other boys in his group were already comfortable with the process, but for him everything was new. His eyes, wide, shifted from place to place. He was almost overcome with awe. And the sound of water splashing, which reminded him of a summer swimming party, contrasted with the whispers and the quiet reverence of the people around him.

Before beginning, the baptist coached him, and explained how to fall backward after the baptismal prayer, how to rise back up, and how to plug his nose with one hand and hold onto the baptist's forearm with the other.

With his right hand raised to the square, the baptist nodded and waited for a name to pop up on the screen in front of him.

A temple worker in white blazer, white tie and white slacks, who sat at a small desk beside the font, returned the nod. On his computer screen, he had a list of hundreds of names of dead people. Each name needed to be marked as baptized before it was sent to the next step in the process. And so, he clicked to make a name appear on a screen in front of the baptist. Then, after each immersion, he clicked again and off the name went to the next rite. Each ritual performed in the temple, baptism being the first, was required for the spirit to enter the presence of God.

For the baptist and the child, each name that appeared on the screen was accompanied by a death date.

The first name was *Glen Henderson*, who died in 1944. The baptist raised his right hand and recited the prayer, saying that he was baptizing the boy "for and in behalf of Glen Henderson, who is dead. In the name of the Father, and of the Son, and of the Holy Ghost. Amen." He held his open right hand against the boy's back, the boy fell backward into the water, and the baptist raised him out again. One baptism was finished. Without delay, the baptist raised his hand to the square again, and began the prayer in behalf of another dead person, then another and another.

Robert Heath, who died in 1899, was the sixth name. Robert Heath, the young professor, teacher, orator, revelator, son, brother, murderer, lunatic, child of God, monster, human. The name did not mean anything to the man or to the boy who did their duties without pause. They carried on until the tenth baptism was finished.

When the tenth was complete, the baptist helped the boy climb the font's steps. Another child, who had sat on the bench with the others, was ready to enter. Ten more dead souls were baptized. This went on and on, not only on that Saturday, but every day except the Lord's Day.

And so doing, they perceived they were saving thousands, ten-thousands, and millions upon millions of souls.

Afterword

This book is a product of trying to not write this book. Writing a book filled with Mormon characters, symbolism, and culture was always in the back of my mind, and though I tried to keep from writing what I wanted to write, I found myself gravitating back to the subject nearly every time I sat down to type.

My sweet wife has urged me to write fiction for many years, an idea that sometimes made me defiant. I am grateful for her support and her patience. I'm grateful for my parents, who have made me who I am, and for my children who have waited patiently, watching me write. I am also thankful to those who gave me their honest feedback about the manuscript. There are so many people in my life who are kind, supportive, and generous, and I hope I have expressed my gratitude enough to everyone privately and publicly.

Now, I suppose I've got this topic out of my system...Perhaps.

Contact The Author

James Elliot

jbluehat@gmail.com

9 781956 707304